# EDGELAND

ALSO BY
JAKE HALPERN & PETER KUJAWINSKI

*Nightfall*

# EDGELAND

## JAKE HALPERN AND PETER KUJAWINSKI

HOT
KEY
BOOKS

First published in Great Britain in 2017 by
HOT KEY BOOKS
80 Furnival St, London W1G 9RE
www.hotkeybooks.com

A CIP catalogue record for this book is available from the British Library.

ISBN: 978–1–4714–0590–7
*also available as an ebook*

Printed and bound by Clays Ltd, St Ives Plc

Hot Key Books is an imprint of Bonnier Zaffre Ltd,
a Bonnier Publishing company
www.bonnierpublishing.com

*To Ari*

The islands of Purgatory lie shrouded in fog.
The dead wait and reflect upon their now-finished lives.
No one laughs. No one sings. No one cries. There is
neither sadness nor joy. It is a solemn place, for the dead
must earn passage to *the kingdom of heaven*.

—*The Common Book: Chapter 6, Verse 12*

# CHAPTER 1

Wren walked along the edge of the known world looking for coins to steal. A few coppers would do. A silver piece would be even better. Her escape fund was almost complete, and soon she'd be sailing for the great spice-trading city of Ankora.

Her eyes darted across the rocks, searching for the dull gleam of metal. She had been doing this for so many years that it had become second nature. It was forbidden, of course, but she had a worthy goal. Leaving Edgeland would mean the end of stealing—from the living, and the dead.

A spray of mist dampened Wren's face as she gazed off into the Drain: a massive, circular waterfall, almost thirty miles in diameter, into which all the water in the ocean drained. This close, it was hard to see anything but the churning water. On rare occasions, you could see the far side of the waterfall.

Today the late-afternoon sky was dark with clouds, and visibility was low. After a few seconds, Wren turned away. She wasn't there to gape.

She was there to work.

Wren stood on the uppermost level of the Ramparts, an ancient seawall that circled the Drain. There was a road on top with lookouts, and vents at the bottom that allowed water to pass through but kept big ships from being pulled in. Most of the ships that sailed through these waters were headed to Edgeland—a nearby island, which sat just a few miles from the Drain. Wren lived here. It was composed almost entirely of bone houses, which blessed and processed dead bodies.

A burst of chanting grabbed Wren's attention. Up ahead, a group of religious pilgrims had gathered around a priest. Such scenes were typical on the Ramparts. Suns and Shadows both believed that the Drain was the gateway to the afterlife, and both sent their dead into the Drain. They threw coins into the water, too, hoping the bits of gold and silver would reach their loved ones.

Once in a while, when Wren was feeling lonely, she'd flick a coin into the Drain for her mother, who'd died four years ago in a boating accident. Wren sometimes liked to picture her down there, in a happy place glimmering with mist. But today she had no time to daydream.

She gave the pilgrims a wide berth as she passed by. They were Shadows, wearing their customary silver prayer robes. It was unusual to see them during the daylight hours.

"*SINNERS!*" their priest yelled. "*Turn from evil and embrace the Shadow, so we can drown the Serpent of Fear.*"

The others punched the air with their fists and chanted: "THE SHADOW! THE SHADOW! THE SHADOW!"

They began passing a cloth-swaddled bundle. It was a

baby. Eventually, it came to rest in the hands of the priest—a tall, fat man in a shimmering cloak and ornate silver crown.

The priest's name was Friderik, though his enemies called him "Fat Freddy." Wren didn't know him personally, but she'd seen him and his followers. People said he was a "firebrand," but as far as Wren could tell, Friderik was nothing more than a bully in fancy robes. To provoke the Suns, he gathered his followers during daylight hours and led them in loud prayers.

Fat Freddy was playing a dangerous game. In this part of the world—thousands of miles due south from the Polar North—the Rule of Light was strictly observed: During the seventy-two hours of day, the Suns ruled and could do as they pleased, while the seventy-two hours of night belonged to the Shadows.

Fat Freddy and his Shadows didn't even glance at Wren as she walked past. She looked like nothing more than a poor Sun girl, her frayed yellow cloak draped over her head and body. They would have been shocked to see that the cloak's inner lining was silver, which meant she could pass as a Shadow when she wanted. It was illegal to own such a robe even worse than Fat Freddy's disobeying the Rule of Light—but for a thief like Wren, a reversible cloak came in handy.

Wren could still see Fat Freddy and his Shadows in the distance when she stopped abruptly, blinking away the mist. A coin glittered near the Rampart's edge. Usually, Wren found coppers, but *this* was a dinar from the Eastern Crags—made of gold and inset with a jadeite nugget. It was a once-in-a-lifetime find.

Wren glanced around, looking for the sentries who patrolled the Ramparts. As she knew too well, it was a serious crime to steal from the dead. And the sentries were hardened men—who'd be all too happy to lop off a few of her fingers in the name of justice. Thankfully, none were in sight.

The gold dinar rested on a flat stone engraved with the most famous mantra from the holy Common Book:

## DROWN THE SERPENT OF FEAR.

Both Suns and Shadows believed that you had to cleanse yourself of fear before entering purgatory—the great waiting room before heaven. This particular mantra was everywhere: etched on flags, painted on the sides of buildings, even tattooed on the legs and backs of the devout. Before becoming a thief, Wren had worked at a bone house where bodies were blessed before their voyage to the Drain. She'd been forced to write this mantra over and over on the bottom of funeral rafts. Merely looking at it made her hand cramp.

Only a guardrail separated Wren from the dinar. She glanced around and saw no one. Wren knelt down, as if praying, and pressed the palm of her hand against a rotting wooden slat. Her robe fell back, revealing a scratched-up brown arm. On her wrist was a bracelet, a simple rope loop with a talisman on it—a wooden figurine of a girl that her mother had carved.

Wren pressed harder against the guardrail until the wood began to give. A post cracked, allowing her arm to snake through. She kept reaching, reaching, reaching—until her finger touched the coin. She dragged it toward her. When the dinar was safely in her fist, she let her eyes wander down into the Drain itself, which was obscured in mist. *Thank goodness for that*. They said if you gazed too deeply into the Drain, you'd lose your mind.

Time to move.

Wren put the dinar in her cloak pocket, along with a few copper coins she'd found, and walked quickly back along the Ramparts. She couldn't stop smiling. She pictured herself standing on a beautiful ocean clipper, sails full of wind, bound for the fragrant streets of Ankora. She'd find the man who'd come looking for her years ago when she'd first arrived in Edgeland. Maybe she had a wealthy inheritance waiting for her and a great big extended family, too. All right, so maybe that was too much to hope for. But still, any family at all— even a distant third cousin—would be better than nothing.

Which is what she had now.

Nothing.

On the island of Edgeland, the mix of young beggars and thieves who lived in tunnels beneath the ground were called Graylings, because their skin was often gray with dirt and grime. It was a miserable life. Wren had to cut her hair, almost to the scalp, to keep the lice away. But not for much longer.

Wren kicked at the pebble-strewn ground in front of her.

*I wish Alec would come with me. But why would he?* Alec had parents, cousins, family of all types and flavors, and a good position at a prestigious bone house. It was a miracle that they were friends.

The bell signaling the ferry's departure for Edgeland began to clang, interrupting her thoughts. A long, steep set of stairs led to the ferry landing below, where crowds of mourners had begun to line up. They were a mishmash of Suns from every corner of the world—pale-skinned boys in turbans from the Eastern Crags, old men in chain mail from the Highlands, and women from the Jade Archipelago in shimmering green cloaks.

The bell clanged again, followed by a burst of excited shouts and cries. At the bottom of the stairs, a mob of angry Suns surrounded Fat Freddy's entourage.

"We're not going anywhere!" shouted a small man with a hawkish nose and a razor-thin beard along his chin. "We do *not* submit to Suns!" Wren recognized him. His name was Dorman—one of Freddy's loudest supporters.

"You have no right to be here during daylight!" hollered one of the Suns. He pushed Dorman, knocking him backward. Soon, others were shoving, too.

"PROTECT THE BABY!" screamed Dorman. "JOIN RANKS!"

Fat Freddy's followers formed a tight circle around a small woman who was holding the baby.

"Separate yourselves!" yelled a red-faced sentry, who was standing in the thick of the mob and trying desperately to keep the peace. "Separate yourselves!"

Wren grimaced and made her way down the stairs, looking for a place where she could jump off and slide down the embankment to the landing below. The stairs made several sharp turns and, at one of these bends, she came upon three Suns, their gold robes smeared with blotches of red.

Wren stopped short. *Those are bloodstains.* A big, bull-necked bald man grabbed her robe and pulled her toward him.

"You didn't see us!" he hissed, so close that she could

feel his spittle landing on her cheeks. Then he pushed her roughly away. The other two men paused, as if trying to decide whether to attack her.

Wren eyed the red marks the man had left on the shoulder and sleeves of her robe.

"I never saw you," she whispered, nodding her head.

The men rushed past, revealing the body of a man lying on the ground. It was Fat Freddy. A knife was lodged right below his heart. His watery eyes strained to look at Wren. Fat Freddy was alive, but he wouldn't be for long.

Wren glanced down at the sleeves of her robe. She began rolling them up frantically, trying to hide the blood.

Seconds later, Dorman appeared at the base of the stairs.

"MASTER!" he shouted. "MY PRIEST!" He looked up at Wren, his face frozen in shock.

More Shadows appeared next to him, looking at Fat Freddy and then at Wren.

Dorman pointed a finger at Wren. *"That grayling girl did this!"* he yelled. *"Murderer!"*

Wren turned and sprinted back up the stairs, willing herself to move faster than she ever had before.

# CHAPTER 2

Two hours later and several miles away, Alec heaved the oars of his skiff and then glanced back over his shoulder. The furrier's ship was getting closer. It had four masts bearing giant, billowing yellow sails. They'd come to float their dead into the Drain, riding the Fourteen-Year Tide. And they were right on schedule.

They'd see him soon. *But would it be soon enough?* Alec had to keep rowing—keep holding his place—that was the key. If he stopped, the currents would grab his tiny boat and fling it into the Drain. The Ramparts were a fail-safe only for bigger vessels: clippers, knarrs, and brigantines.

The skiff rolled heavily to starboard, and Alec yanked on the oars. Frothing whitecaps roiled and splashed around him. He gritted his teeth. *If Wren could see me now, she'd laugh, until she realized how serious this was—then she'd smack me.*

Up to this moment, Alec's had been a quiet existence, spent mainly indoors; a stark contrast to Wren's life on the streets. And now, here he was, alone, in a small boat, battling the

Drain's vicious current. *I'm still the only boat out here*, Alec thought with satisfaction. He had calculated that the furriers would arrive in Edgeland *today*. And if he could persuade them to use House Aron for their funerals . . . well . . . Sami Aron would be very pleased. The coffers at House Aron were shrinking, and the furriers paid in sunstones and polar diamonds; it'd be the richest haul anyone had seen in years.

*What'll my father say when he hears the news?*

For a second, Alec smiled. His parents were wealthy landowners from the north. His two older brothers had been explorers; they'd crossed the high peaks of the Jagged Teeth Mountains and returned with chests full of gold nuggets. But Alec's father thought that he was too small and timid for such a life—and often told his mother so.

"But how can you tell?" asked his mother. "He's only a child."

His father scoffed. "He's too frightened to walk down the stairs to the cellar by himself," he said. "Alec's a clever boy, but he's no explorer. And he knows it."

*And he knows it*. That was the worst part—because his father was right. Alec *was* afraid of the cellar and the Jagged Teeth Mountains and a great many other things as well.

So, at the age of eight, Alec had been sent off to apprentice at House Aron, to begin a life of reading and praying. And then he'd been forgotten. Well, not exactly forgotten. His parents wrote him letters, filled with pleasantries and bits of news. *It's been a cold winter . . . Your brother has a new horse . . . We can't visit this summer, but maybe the next.* Meanwhile, Alec had done well at House Aron. He picked up foreign languages with ease and worked tirelessly to arrange funerals. Now clients arrived and often asked for him by name. He was building a reputation. Not that his parents noticed. But they would soon . . . They'd have to. Books and reading be damned. Alec had snagged a great, big haul of sunstones—even more valuable than gold nuggets. *What do you think of that, Father?*

The ship was close now. Alec stood, dropped his oars, and began waving his arms. "Over here!" he screamed, willing his voice to rise over the sound of the ocean. "OVER HERE! I AM THE GHOST-CHILD!"

Years ago, Alec had memorized Witold's epic funeral ode, in which a *ghost-child*—a flicker of a boy—rows across the rapids of the Drain, in a skiff, to greet the furrier captain and escort him to purgatory. The poem was beloved by furriers, mainly because it was filled with descriptions of epic battles they'd won. The ghost-child is the hero, a boy of unrivaled bravery, who accompanies the sailors all the way to heaven. Some furriers even engraved the poem's verses onto the prows of their ships. At first, Alec believed his plan to pose as the ghost-child was clever, though less so now that he was close to capsizing.

Alec's boat lurched forward, and the crest of a wave crashed over the gunwales. The starboard oarlock popped open, and the oar was swept overboard. Another wave surged over the bow. Alec lost his footing and fell backward, grazing his head against the boat's wooden ribs. Blood began to trickle down his pale forehead. The boat wallowed in the sea, wrenched in opposite directions by the strong currents of the Drain.

*The furriers. Where are the damn furriers?*

He looked around, momentarily confused. Where was the ship? But then he saw it—alongside him now—the massive ship and its billowing yellow sails. Far above on the deck, a man with a long white beard and a spyglass was pointing at Alec.

Someone from the ship flung a rope. It arched up and away and came down expertly across the skiff. Alec grabbed the rope, wrapped it several times around his arms, and jumped into the water. He and the rope were pulled up to the deck, where he collapsed in a sodden heap. The skiff was quickly taken by the current and sped toward the Drain.

The furrier with the spyglass looked down at Alec, arms folded across his chest. A deeply weathered face and a profusion of sunspots betrayed his age, but he was still powerfully built, his figure made more imposing by the thick, fur-lined slicks that covered him from neck to toe.

The ship plunged into a deep trough. Alec gagged. Locks of his braided blond hair dripped seawater onto his face.

"If you puke on my deck, I'll throw you off," said the furrier. "I don't care if my crew thinks you're the reincarnation of the ghost-child or not."

Alec nodded. Although he spoke the dialect of the Far North—as well as seven other languages—he refrained from speaking right now. *Never cross a furrier.* Everyone knew that.

"I am Isidro," the man said. "Let me hazard a guess—you're from one of the bone houses."

Alec nodded again.

Isidro shook his head. "Which one?"

Alec cleared his throat before speaking. "House Aron," he rasped. "I'm Alec."

Isidro chuckled darkly and exchanged knowing looks with a nearby crew member. "The first and the finest Sun house. Isn't that right? Is Sami Aron still in charge?"

Alec nodded with satisfaction. He crawled to a nearby wooden rail and rose to his feet, gripping the rail for balance. The fact that Isidro knew about House Aron wasn't entirely surprising. Sami Aron was the latest scion of the family who'd run the house for more than five hundred years. They were renowned for their ability to hold Edgeland's largest and most complex funerals for Suns.

"You're a fool to risk your life," said Isidro. He paused to spit over the rail of the ship. "Still, you're brave. Our dead appreciate that."

*Brave.* Alec puffed out his chest, but it only seemed to emphasize how small he was. He returned to his usual slouch. It didn't matter—he was thrilled. In his entire life, no one had ever called him brave—except perhaps his mother, on the day she'd shipped him off to Edgeland.

Isidro reached into his sealskin and took out a flask that glimmered with rubies and sapphires. Alec eyed the flask in wonder. The furriers truly were rich. And soon some of those riches would belong to House Aron. Isidro took a swig, then smacked his lips and returned the flask to his coat.

"I never much cared for this part of the world," said Isidro, glancing over the boat's stern. It was an imposing ship, with over a dozen sails and several levels, including a main deck, a quarterdeck, and a gun deck. Sealskin-clad deckhands moved about silently. "The daylight fades too quickly here, and you rub shoulders with Shadows." He shuddered. "Give me the Polar North's fourteen years of sun and a stiff wind at my back."

Alec often heard statements like that from Suns who'd never actually met any Shadows. In general, Suns believed that truth and goodness flourished only in the daylight, while Shadows thought that sunlight—and even torchlight—encouraged vanity and greed. Darkness brought humility, they said. It was a never-ending debate everywhere, but especially on Edgeland.

Isidro glanced at Alec, as if suddenly remembering that he was still there. "Yours is a famous house," he remarked. "In my youth, I knew a song about House Aron, something about an ember shining away the night . . ."

"That's right," said Alec. "Ember Aron founded the house—she was a great scholar."

"Never cared much for books," said Isidro with a shrug. "Spent my life hunting for gems."

*I know the type,* thought Alec. *My father would sooner use a book to start a campfire than to read.*

Isidro paused, looking off to sea, then turned to address Alec. "I have thirty-five dead men, one woman, and a child here," Isidro said. "All in ice. We have scows, so we'll only need House Aron to do the blessings and send the bodies into the Drain." The furriers only visited Edgeland once every fourteen years. In the interim, anyone who died was preserved in ice, so they could have a proper funeral and be sent into the Drain at a later time.

"The sun's going down," said Alec. "Are your dead still frozen solid?"

Isidro frowned. "They're thawing fast now that we've come south. We'll need to go over before sunset." He paused to glance at the setting sun. "Perhaps ten hours left. Can you do it?"

"We *will* do it," replied Alec.

"You should know that I am the Elder Furrier," said Isidro.

Alec paused before responding. The Elder Furrier escorted their people into the next life. Isidro would go over the Drain with the others. It was an ancient tradition, rarely observed in modern times. *I'm expected to help him commit suicide. This is the polite life that my parents wanted for me?*

"You'll need poison," said Alec finally.

"Yes, yes," replied Isidro. He tugged at his white beard. "So, *Alec the Ghost-Child*"—he paused to laugh—"lead us to your pier."

Alec ran to the bow and stared off toward Edgeland. The closest shore was lined with warehouses that stored the dead. Farther inland, on a great hill, was the Mount, where the temples stood. Alec focused on the island's biggest pier, filled with Suns enjoying their last hours of light. He strained his eyes and found who he was looking for.

Ellie, his assistant, waited for him near the end of the pier. Alec reached into his jacket and pulled out a pocket mirror, which he aimed at the setting sun. Once it produced a bead of light, he carefully rotated the mirror so the light shone onto the pier.

"Come on, Ellie, look up," Alec whispered.

14

# CHAPTER 3

Ellie was tall and fair-eyed, with freckles sprayed across her cheeks. Her waist-length red hair hadn't been dyed since the winter solstice—nearly a year ago—and blond roots were showing. At ten years old, she was still a whiff. In Edgeland, it was said that whiffs carried the "stench of birth," which could easily taint the dead. For these reasons, those younger than twelve were required to have their hair dyed red so they could be easily identified. Whiffs were also supposed to stay indoors, but today, Ellie had a special task.

Ellie worshiped Alec, who had also started as an apprentice. Like her, Alec came from a devout and wealthy Sun family. If she did well, she might follow in his footsteps.

As Ellie paced back and forth, she was careful to keep away from a nearby group of lower-class servants. A few of them, who appeared to be of marrying age, were washing clothes against the coarse sand of the beach, while others yanked lampreys from the rocks.

"Killed ol' Fat Freddy with a poke of a knife," said one of

the chambermaids. She smacked her fist against her belly to mimic the blow. "Killed 'im and left him for dead right on the Ramparts path—in plain view. They say it was a grayling girl wit' scarred arms and a shaved head who done it. But they'll find 'er. Half the island's lookin'. They're already startin' to search the descenders."

"Witchery," said a silver-haired servant as she pinched off the head of a lamprey and crammed the wriggling body into her mouth. "Ain't that obvious? A lone grayling couldn't kill a big fat man like that on 'er own. Musta used black magic to get the job done."

"Th' Shadows will be out fer blood," said the chambermaid. "I heard people in their neighborhoods are already takin' up steel."

"Th' fat priest deserved it," cackled the old woman, but she was immediately shushed by the chambermaid, who whispered and pointed at Ellie.

"What's a whiff doing out here?" the chambermaid called.

Ellie's face went red. "I have special permission."

"*Special* permission," echoed the old woman, taking a step closer to Ellie. "Why, you are a special whiff—ain't ya?" She glanced at the others to make sure they were watching and then did an elaborate, fumbling curtsy. The others guffawed.

One of the younger women stopped laughing and gasped. Ellie glanced down and saw a round speck of light dancing on her tunic. Startled, she lifted her eyes to the sea. The yellow sails of a furrier ship were just off Needle Island, and the light was coming from the ship's bow. The young chambermaid scampered backward toward an iron bucket that sat near the edge of the pier. It was filled with fearstones: gray and white pebbles meant to symbolize a person's darkest terrors. The woman picked up a pebble, muttered at it for several seconds, then threw it into the water—drowning it.

Ellie turned to the woman happily. "There's no need for that," she announced. "It's nothing to be afraid of. Something wonderful has happened!" Without waiting for their reaction, Ellie bowed and started running down the pier.

*Alec. It's him. He's done it!*

At the end of the pier, she turned up a narrow alleyway, directly to the back door of House Aron. Several people were gathered there, including grizzled old Butros, the house watchman, and Sami Aron himself.

"What are you doing outside, *whiff*?" demanded Butros. He rested a palm on the flintlock horse pistol fixed to his belt. "Haven't you heard about Fat Freddy's murder? There's bound to be trouble from th' Shadows. What makes you think you can—"

"Enough," interrupted Sami Aron, running a hand across his bald head. "Let her speak. You're Alec's assistant, are you not?"

Ellie nodded.

"Do you bring news?" asked Sami Aron. His large eyes seemed to bore into her. "What has become of Alec's plan?"

"A furrier boat is coming," gasped Ellie, who was still trying to catch her breath. "Alec is with them. They'll be at our pier soon."

"How soon?" asked Sami Aron, leaning toward Ellie.

"Thirty minutes," said Ellie. "Maybe less."

17

"We must hurry," said Sami Aron quietly, almost to himself. No one moved. He turned to Butros. "Get my mourner's cloak, call the Blind, and get the whole House down to the pier—at once. Everything must be *perfect*!"

Butros turned to go, but Sami Aron grabbed him by the shoulder. "Get as many Blind as you can. Their dead will be frozen, and whatever we do, we cannot let those bodies thaw."

# CHAPTER 4

Wren leaned on the ferry railing and watched as the stone warehouses of Edgeland appeared in the distance. The ocean breeze was pleasant against her face. Usually she picked pockets on the ferry, but today she didn't dare. Right now, she considered herself lucky to be alive.

After encountering Fat Freddy's body, she'd run along the Ramparts for almost two miles before reaching another ferry landing. Then she washed the blood off her cloak as best she could, put on the black wig and hat that she always carried with her, and shuffled onto the boat. It was one of the older ferries and moved very slowly, taking almost four hours to make the journey that faster boats made in just one. At least it was an uneventful ride. She was nearly home. And with that gold dinar in her pocket, it wouldn't be home much longer.

"What mischief are *you* up to, my little rat?"

Wren whirled around and saw Crown, a pudgy, red-cheeked smuggler with crooked teeth and a jovial smile. He wore a splendid Sun tunic of pure-spun white wool intertwined with gold thread.

Occasionally, he hired Wren to do small jobs—stealing a key or letters. It was unclear whether Crown was a Sun or a Shadow. Like Wren, he switched between the two. Most people wouldn't dare put on the cloaks of the other religion, but Wren and Crown weren't like other people. They believed in only one thing: survival.

"You scared me!" Wren exclaimed, forcing a smile.

"Got any goodies for me?" Crown asked.

"Maybe," replied Wren. She paused and drew a little closer to him. "Do you have any boats leaving Edgeland soon? I might have enough for a sea voyage."

"There's always room for you," said Crown. He frowned. "I do have expenses, though." Wren knew what this meant—he was about to negotiate. "You've got no papers, I expect. Every day, there are more people to bribe. But there *is* a smuggler's ship at the Incense Merchants' Pier, if you can pay. It leaves at dawn—bound for the Desert Lands. What's that town you want to go to?"

"Ankora," Wren replied. "I'd pay a pretty price, so long as I can leave at dawn."

"You must have found something very valuable," Crown said, raising an eyebrow. "Come by in a few hours and show me what you've gotten your grubby little hands on." He grinned and turned away, wobbling with the sway of the boat.

Wren took a deep breath and felt the air curl its way into her lungs, imagining that she was already on her way to Ankora, a vast city of almost a million people. She pictured herself walking down the narrow streets, spice merchants sitting on either side, hawking vials of pepper, ginger, turmeric, and star anise. She'd start her search there for the bearded man.

A year after she arrived at House Aron—when she was nine years old—the bearded man had visited the Edgeland bone houses, politely asking for a young orphan girl named "In Bryll."

He spoke with a thick southland accent, in which he swallowed the *wr* and *e* in her first name. Few people knew Wren's last name, and the bearded man was turned away. It was weeks later that Butros, the house watchman at House Aron, mentioned the encounter. He remembered little about the visitor, other than his beard and the fact that he claimed to hail from the city of Ankora.

The news was electrifying for Wren. She felt certain that the bearded man was her father, Isaac. He'd left when Wren was six—signed on as third mate on a whaling ship bound for the Polar North. The ship was supposed to be gone for ten months, but two years after its departure, it still hadn't returned. "He'll come back," her mother, Alinka, promised. In fact, Alinka kept on promising this right until the day that she died. And then, well . . . Wren was officially an orphan.

When Butros told her of the visit from the "bearded man," Wren's hopes soared. She searched every nook and cranny on the island, hoping to find him. This wasn't easy to do because whiffs weren't allowed outdoors. She found a wig and dressed as a body washer, wearing a hooded cloak and heeled boots—all of which made her look much older. The watchmen at a few other bone houses remembered the bearded man. "Yes," recalled one. "He had a birthmark on his right cheek." That confirmed it. Her father had a crescent-shaped birthmark above his beard. *It was him*. But it didn't matter: By then, he'd already vanished.

As the ferry approached the dock on Edgeland, Wren could smell the island's scent—a mix of incense, vinegar, and decaying flesh.

Several excited voices began speaking at once.

"Smoke—do you see it?" someone called. "It's a sign—it looks like a serpent in the sky—a drowned serpent."

Wren looked down the main deck of the ferry, where a group of aged Suns stood, wearing the homespun clothing of the northern regions. They were pointing to the highest part of the island—the Mount—a flat expanse occupied by several large temples. Several thin lines of smoke had begun to rise from this area.

Wren gripped the railing and leaned forward. Sometimes Suns lit small fires around the Mount in order to demonstrate the power of light. It was a bad sign. Tensions were running high. Wren guessed that word was already out about Fat Freddy. News must have traveled on the faster ferry.

When the ferry docked, Wren hurried down the gangplank toward a nearby maze of rickety wooden shacks. The "Shakes" is what they called this mud-splattered marketplace where the island's poor came to buy, sell, and rob one another. It was also the name they gave to the hovels they lived in, which rattled and shook in even the lightest wind.

Wren began to relax once she was slopping down the Shakes's muddy lanes, amidst the throngs of bedraggled old

22

women and stray dogs. There were also quite a few graylings—begging for scraps of food and looking for coins to steal. Wren tried hard *not* to look like a grayling. She kept her cloak clean and always washed her face and hands, even if the rest of her was dirty, because those were the parts of her body people were most likely to see.

Wren passed the fruit stalls, the incense kiosks, and the hut where the old man made funeral kites from pigs' intestines. The Shakes was one of the few places where Suns and Shadows mingled—the Rule of Light didn't mean much here.

Wren walked to the end of a lane, then across a dust-covered field toward a one-room hut. There was a reason it stood by itself. It was next to a foul-smelling marsh, making it a perfect place for those who wished to be left alone. Wren ducked through the small front door of the hut.

"Look what the dead dragged in," said an old man in a tattered white tunic. As always, he was slouching in a rickety chair and chewing a piece of marsh grass. "You look like hell."

"Thanks, Irv. So do you." Wren removed her hat and black wig, revealing a closely shorn head and chestnut-colored eyes that rested above high cheekbones. She was the same age as Alec, but the strain on her face made her look older.

Irv's place was simple. The only ornament on the walls was a small painting of the great Shadow prophet, Shade, who appeared serious and brooding. Shade was a contemporary of Ember Aron, and had lived and died centuries ago. He had founded several of the Shadow bone houses. For his part, Irv wasn't especially religious, but he was a Shadow and a painting of Shade was a good-luck talisman.

Irv's shack was essentially a storage shed: floor-to-ceiling shelves lined with dirty paper bags. Each bag contained four so-called bricks of life—the dietary staple of those who lived in the Shakes. The bricks were made of baked flour, grass, clay, and a sprinkling of sugar. If you ate too many bricks, you'd die—the clay would poison you. If you didn't eat *enough* bricks, you would also die—of starvation. And this conundrum summarized the sort of world in which Wren lived.

Wren walked to a blanket hanging in the far corner and pulled it up, revealing a wide tube that led down into the descenders, a network of old, forgotten tunnels and pipes below Edgeland. She peered in and saw torchlight flickering below, then turned back to Irv and flipped him one of the coppers she'd taken from the Ramparts.

"This settles us for the week, right?"

He tilted his head in acknowledgment. "What happened to your sandals?"

Wren looked down. They were smeared with Fat Freddy's blood. "Walking through the Shakes," she said, rolling her eyes. "Must've stepped in some pig guts."

"Let me know if you see anything down there," said Irv.

"See anything?" Wren frowned. "Should I be expecting company?"

The old man shrugged. "Someone killed a Shadow priest— what's his name, big fat fella—Freddy? Then they started fightin' on the Mount again." Irv glanced at the picture of Shade on the wall, as if nervous about sharing this information in the prophet's presence.

"I saw the smoke," Wren replied.

"It's not just that," Irv continued. "They say a *grayling* killed Fat Freddy." He saw her worried face and nodded sympathetically. "I know, it's unfair. Graylings are always the first ones they blame. They'll probably fight on the Mount for a few hours, and that'll be the end of it. Still, be careful down there. They're lookin' for an excuse to clear out the descenders and kill thievin' graylings."

Wren fell silent. She looked at the picture of Shade and the bricks of life. At that moment, she hated Edgeland more than ever.

"I don't know why they even bother," continued Irv. "You know what they say about graylings: They never grow old because they—"

"All die young," finished Wren.

"Yup," said Irv. "It's hard scrappin' for food and livin' belowground, but you know that. It's a mean life. Never did see a grayling live to be fully grown." He sighed heavily. "Yes sir, people sure do hate your lot."

"But why?" pressed Wren. "Why do they hate us so much?"

Irv rocked back in his chair. "Well, ya got the stink of birth on you, like all whiffs do. Only it's worse because, on top of that, graylings are troublemakers—like you—who got kicked out of their bone houses. And let's be honest, most of ya are thieves." He cackled. "I like troublemakers, but I'm not like most folks."

Wren gave him a wry smile. "I guess what I'm asking is, how'd all this start?"

Irv stood up and walked over to Wren. He peered down

the descender. "I reckon it's because Edgeland's a place for the dead, or the nearly dead. Old folks don't like to be reminded of youth. And graylings are a combination of the two worst things: being a child and not following the rules of th' all-powerful bone houses." His kindly face creased into a smile, and he patted her on the shoulder. "Don't worry, Wrennie, you won't be young forever."

# CHAPTER 5

Wren wondered whether she should tell Irv she was about to leave Edgeland for good. After all, he was probably the closest thing she had to a parent. Well, not a parent exactly. Maybe a weaselly old uncle? In any case, she got the sense that he actually cared about her. So long as she paid her rent, of course.

Wren smiled at Irv and gave his hand a quick squeeze. It felt like a bunch of bones covered in dry paper. That would have to suffice as good-bye for now.

Wren walked over to the descender that led down to her lair. She pushed herself into the smooth tube, propping her back against one side and her feet against the other. A slip would mean death, but she wasn't scared—she'd been clambering in and out of these pipes for years. No one knew *every* twist and turn, but Wren could enter the descenders at Irv's shack and emerge easily anywhere on the island.

About ten feet from the bottom, Wren jumped. The bronze hummed when she landed, sending a number of rats skittering. She stood up easily in this massive tube. The walls were caked with dirt, ash, and crude chalk drawings of boats, knives, and coins. Wren had drawn some of the pictures herself. Others were from the distant past. There were sections of the descenders, deeper down, with ornate renderings of three-headed wolves, flying rats, and giant snakes with claws and scissor-like tongues. Graylings competed with one another to create the wildest graffiti.

Irv had hung lamps every ten feet in this section. They swung from bronze hooks jutting from the ceiling. There were always drafts in the descenders—air rushing from one network of pipes to another—and the lanterns creaked rhythmically. Irv had also built gates that restricted access to this specific descender. For these services he charged Wren a copper a week. He was robbing her, of course, but given that she was a thief, it was hard to complain.

Wren walked past a stack of several dozen metal urns that held Irv's stockpile of black-market lantern oil. After another thirty feet or so, she came upon the nest of blankets that she used as a bed. Next to it stood a wobbly little table with a few candles, two rusting knives, and some half-eaten bricks of life.

Home.

She shuffled the blankets. Two large, shiny cockroaches ambled away. Wren watched them go with a disinterested air. She had long been accustomed to their presence. The only thing she didn't like was when they crawled across her face at night. Even the rats that lived in the descenders respected her personal space better than that.

Wren sat down cross-legged and rested her back against the cool metal of the descender. She glanced at the scars on her forearms. Graylings fought often in the descenders. They used knives, or whatever jagged shards of metal they could get hold of, while scrapping for food, coins, and territory. Wren had been in more than a few such scuffles, and had the marks to prove it.

She absentmindedly rubbed the wooden figurine that was strapped around her wrist. The figurine was smooth from years of handling. Her mother, Alinka, had carved it just before she'd died. Wren could still picture the cottage they'd lived in: blackened fireplace, wood rafters that smelled like smoke, and clay walls that went muddy in the rainy season. Out front was a porch, with three rocking chairs.

Wren had been sitting in one of those chairs when two elderly women from the Sisterhood of the Suns came to the house. They explained that Alinka had drowned when her boat capsized. It was a small ferry. Her mother took it every Sunday, on her weekly trip to the market.

After that, everything was a blur. The women from the Sisterhood asked if she had any family—aunts, uncles, grandparents. Wren shook her head. For as long as she could remember, she had no other family but her parents. Eventually, like so many orphans, she was shipped off to Edgeland to serve at one of the great bone houses.

Wren was soon reciting prayers, polishing amulets, and writing **DROWN THE SERPENT OF FEAR** on funeral rafts. She met Alec, Ellie, and the other apprentices. She studied the Common Book. She settled into her new life. And then the bearded man—her father—had come for her. Only they missed each other. When she couldn't find him on Edgeland,

Wren was determined to chase him back to Ankora. But that would cost money, which she didn't have.

So she took a risk.

Late one night, she broke the most sacred rule at House Aron: She stole a diamond ring from the finger of a dead woman. Sami Aron found out and banished her.

Wren had been living in the descenders with the rats and cockroaches ever since. It was a lonely life. Sometimes, when she couldn't sleep at night, she lay in the darkness and talked to her dead mother, recounting her day—what she'd eaten, where she'd gone, whom she'd chatted with—boring stuff, the kind of talk that only a mother really cared to hear.

Wren used one of the blankets to wipe the bloodstains from her sandals. Then she stood up and reached high toward a hole in the wall: the opening to a small descender, no wider than two fists. She jumped and pulled out a hefty burlap satchel hidden inside. Within the satchel lay several hundred coins of different sizes and denominations, along with loose jewels she'd pried from stolen amulets.

A shout broke the silence of the descender.

"ANSWER ME!"

The voice was coming from the other side of the nearest locked gate. Wren put the gold dinar in her satchel and returned it to its hiding place. Then she grabbed one of the rusting knives from her bedside, put it in her robe pocket, and walked over to the gate.

"ANSWER ME!" repeated the voice. "ARE YOU THERE?!"

Wren unlocked the gate and continued along the descender. She snaked her hand into her pocket and clutched the handle of her knife. She was good with a blade and never ventured far into the descenders without one.

Wren kept walking until she came upon Joseph, a grayling with pale white skin and sunken eyes. He was staring into the Plunge—a ten-foot-wide descender that dropped straight down into the earth. Wren had thrown rocks into it without ever hearing them hit bottom. Three months ago, Joseph's older brother, Oscar, made a rope hundreds of feet long and climbed down to search for the treasure that was rumored to lie at the bottom. He never returned. Since then, Joseph had been inconsolable.

A steady current of warm air rose from the Plunge as Wren walked toward Joseph.

"You should go to the surface," she said. She released her grip on the knife. "Take a little food break."

Even in the dim light, Wren could see that Joseph hadn't been eating. His skin was loose along his jawline, and his eyes gleamed yellow.

"I forget to eat," Joseph replied with a shrug. "And I can't take any more bricks from you    it ain't right."

Wren had met Joseph and Oscar soon after she'd been kicked out of House Aron. Back then, they'd all been part of a pack of graylings who nested in descenders beneath the Coffin District. The leader of this pack was a thick-boned brute of a girl named Mira. She took a dislike to Oscar because he was big for his age, and it was clear that someday he'd pose a threat to her. Mira eventually decided to give both brothers the boot. Wren decided to leave with them, but she opted to live on her own so she'd only have to worry about herself. Even so, she stayed friendly with the boys. They shared water and bread. And, in a pinch, they fought together. On one occasion, three older graylings attacked Oscar in a remote descender, and Wren—who'd been nearby—jumped into the fray to help him. It was how she'd gotten some of the scars on her arms.

Wren turned her attention back to Joseph, who was staring at her with glassy, vacant eyes.

"Listen," said Wren. "You *need* to eat."

"Oscar's coming back soon," Joseph said. "I know he hears me . . ." He ran the dirty rag of his shirt across his nose. "We're a team, you see? I can't pick pockets on my own."

Wren nodded sympathetically. Life on Edgeland was cruel to graylings. She hurried back to her stash, grabbed a handful of silvers, and pressed them into Joseph's hand.

"Take these," she whispered. "They'll keep you for a few months if you're careful."

Joseph stared at the coins in his hand, then nodded solemnly. "Thank you," he said. "I'll share these with Oscar when he comes back."

Wren turned away, ashamed of the tears filling her eyes. Oscar was likely dead, and Joseph might soon be as well, if he didn't start eating. Edgeland chewed up graylings and spit them out. She had to leave—soon.

Then, rather suddenly, she thought of Alec. Earlier in the day she'd planned on saying good-bye to him, but now—with everyone looking for her—the idea seemed rather foolhardy. But this was Alec. She couldn't leave without saying good-bye.

# CHAPTER
# 6

Alec stood on a raised wooden platform at House Aron's pier, facing the furrier's ship. He'd pulled it off. He'd done something just as glorious as returning home from the Jagged Teeth Mountains with chests of gold. People all over the world revered the bone houses of Edgeland. To have a child working at such a house was a blessing for the parents—especially if that child succeeded grandly, as he'd just done.

Alec glanced back at the crowd that had come to gawk at the Polar North's legendary voyagers. They watched in openmouthed astonishment as the magnificent furrier vessel moored alongside House Aron's dock. Several were friends from other bone houses, and he felt their envious glances as he stood at the middle of the platform, doing his best to appear dignified.

Even though his velvet funeral robe fit him well, beneath it Alec still looked young and scrawny, which was deeply embarrassing to him. Luckily, his fine golden hair contained no trace of red, so he couldn't be mistaken for a whiff. His hair was braided close to the scalp in straight, orderly rows, highlighting his soft, smooth face.

A loud clank rang out from the ship, and the crowd fell silent. Moments later, a wooden crane on the deck swiveled, and its winch boom swung out toward the pier. Alec's eyes were on the cargo that dangled from the crane's rope—a net holding a ten-foot cube of solid ice. The sea ice was cloudy and pale green, but Alec could still see the shape of a dead furrier entombed inside. He might have died ten months ago or ten years ago—either was possible.

Despite the heat, Sami Aron wore his splendid set of rabbit-fur funeral robes. His expression was appropriately grave, though his eyes twinkled with the cheer of imminent wealth.

It took nearly an hour for all the blocks of ice to be lowered to the pier. When this was done, Alec began to recite the Sun Requiem. All eyes were on him, House Aron's shining star. Alec could read a hymn once and, like magic, know the words and melody by heart. In addition to speaking half a dozen languages, he was able to decipher ancient hieroglyphs. In theory, Alec would return home to his family at eighteen, but Sami Aron had no heir, or siblings, which meant that Alec was a candidate to inherit House Aron. Alec thought about this possibility at least once or twice a day.

When Alec finished the chant, two rows of bare-chested, thickly muscled pallbearers marched through the crowd. They were the Blind and—in Edgeland—they were the people who carried the dead. It was believed that the Blind were immune from the temptations of the devil because they could not see. In order to join the Blind, they agreed to sew their eyelids shut. In the absence of sight, many of the Blind developed a keen sense of smell. It was said they could detect the scent of pickles on someone's breath from across a crowded room.

It was fortunate that there were so many Blind on hand: It took six of them to lift each block of ice. Drawn by the prospect of hefty payments and the prestige of carrying furriers, nearly two hundred had come to work at the pier. Slowly they began marching back to House Aron. As they walked, the Blind made a series of shrill, birdlike squawks. Like bats, they navigated by listening to the way sound traveled. Alec and Sami followed, along with other workers from House Aron.

Alec glanced at the furrier's ship one last time. He frowned. The funeral scows lashed to the side were at least thirty feet long. Scows longer than the twenty-foot vents beneath the Ramparts could get lodged sideways and stuck. Alec would need to discuss this with Isidro.

The funeral procession snaked through the narrow cobblestone streets. As Alec and Sami rounded a corner, a small black cat darted across their path. Seconds later, two graylings, dressed in ashen-colored rags and wielding knives, scampered after it. One of them turned, bared its teeth, and hissed at them before disappearing down an adjoining alleyway. Seeing this grayling made Alec think of Wren and the wretched way she lived in the passageways beneath the city. It gave him a pang of guilt. He could do more for her. He *should* do more for her.

"The graylings grow bolder," said Sami Aron, shaking his head. "They used to come out only at night—the Shadows' problem. Now something will have to be done."

Alec nodded gravely. *Something will have to be done.* What did that mean?

"I'm sure you've heard that Fat Freddy was murdered," continued Sami. "On the Ramparts. Of course he deserved it, but there'll be trouble." He sighed. "A filthy grayling killed him."

Alec stiffened, but still he managed to utter the response that Sami Aron expected: "The young have no wisdom."

"Except for you," Sami said, stepping closer and placing a hand on Alec's shoulder. "Fortune has smiled upon you. I always believed that you'd bring me luck."

Alec shrugged slightly, embarrassed but pleased by the praise.

"Well done with the furriers," Sami Aron said. "Keep this up, and who knows how high you may rise."

Warmth flooded Alec's face as he took this in.

Suddenly, a whooshing noise came from a descender that jutted out from a nearby wall, followed by a gust of smoky air.

Sami Aron jerked his head toward the smoke. "Hmm," he said. "Perhaps the Shadows are hunting for that grayling— trying to smoke out the rat."

Alec did not reply. *What if Sami is right? Wren might be down there right now.*

# CHAPTER

# 7

The Blind carried the furriers to House Aron's basement, a cool, cave-like room large enough to house a hundred bodies. Today, the room was so cold that Alec could see his breath as he walked among the ice slabs. Massive candles lined the walls, revealing the words etched into the stone: **DROWN THE SERPENT OF FEAR**.

On the far wall, there was an ornate painting of the Sunlit Glade, the name for the Sun heaven. Alec's mother and his nursemaid both talked about this mythical place. Supposedly it was full of dangling vines, tall grass, and sumptuous fruit. All Sun children grew up on these tales. *Be good and you'll go to the Sunlit Glade one day.*

Shadows called their heaven the Moonlit Beach. It was a separate paradise, reserved only for Shadows. The two religions insisted on dividing everything up—even the afterlife. Of course, Shadows believed the Moonlit Beach was far superior to the Sunlit Glade. They said the beach air smelled of juniper and just a touch of its sand provided everlasting joy.

But first, everyone had to go to purgatory.

In the Common Book, the islands of purgatory were described as desolate and empty isles where the dead waited until they were ready to enter heaven. There were two separate islands within a stone's throw of each other: one for Suns and one for Shadows.

"Don't talk too much about purgatory," Sami Aron had told Alec and the other apprentices. "If clients ask, just say they won't be there for long." Instead, Sami Aron urged everyone to talk about the Sunlit Glade and the lush, green heaven that awaited them. "Give them lots of details. It'll give them comfort."

Ember Aron—the founder of their house—was famous for saying: *In the face of the unknown, give them comfort.*

Alec walked slowly through the basement with a lantern in hand. He paused in front of a piercingly blue-green slab of ice—so solid and massive it could have been hewn directly from an iceberg. The man inside was holding up his right hand, as if warding off attackers. On his wrist was a hefty gold bracelet, which appeared to be encrusted with diamonds. Alec smiled, congratulating himself again for leading the furriers to House Aron.

He peered closer. There were water bubbles in the ice around the man's arm—a telltale sign that the ice was melting.

Alec moved up to get a better look at the furrier's face. What he saw almost made him gag. The furrier's eyes were bulging and his mouth was open, as if he'd been frozen mid-scream. In the middle of his mouth, a purple tongue stuck out like a limb.

"*I* killed that one."

Startled, Alec whirled around. Isidro stood in the shadows several feet away, looking older and grayer than he had on the ship.

"He was a thief," said Isidro, nodding at the furrier. "Stealing is a grave dishonor to our ancestors. Murder can be explained—the heat of passion, and so on. But stealing . . ." He shook his head. "Stealing merits a more painful death."

Alec turned away from the body and stepped toward Isidro. "I'm sorry to disturb you," he said. "But as we left for House Aron, I saw that your funeral boats are long enough to get stuck in the vents. It rarely happens, but . . . still . . . we can provide shorter ones."

Isidro considered this for a moment. "That is fine, but for one exception. My body must be in the scow I built with my own hands. I dreamed that I will need it in purgatory."

The furrier motioned for Alec to follow him and walked to a slab that was larger than the others. Alec raised his lantern and saw not one, but two figures encased in ice. One was a woman; the other was a child. The woman was holding the child tightly to her chest.

"My daughter and grandson are joining me," said Isidro. He straightened up and squared his shoulders, then dropped his eyes to the stone floor.

"I'm sorry," replied Alec.

"The cold killed them," he said. "People think furriers scoff at the snow and ice. But it kills us, too."

Alec said nothing. During awkward silences, it was tempting to speak—to fill the void with babble or by quoting prayers. But sometimes people needed silence.

Isidro rubbed his chin thoughtfully, as if he'd come to a long-awaited decision. "There is something I'd ask you for," he said. "I need two more amulets, like this one. Lola—my daughter—made me promise that I'd get them . . . right before she died."

Isidro reached behind his head and unfastened a woven metal rope from his neck. A delicate onyx amulet dangled from the end. It was about five inches long, made in the shape of a curling ocean wave. Isidro opened it, revealing a tiny serpent within. Alec studied the amulet carefully. The workmanship was mesmerizing. As it caught the light, it looked like the wave was crashing.

"This is how I want the other two," said Isidro, handing it to Alec. "Exact copies."

Alec turned the amulet and traced its contours. "I've never seen an amulet like this," he said. "Still, if anybody has copies, House Aron does. We have the largest reserves of amulets among the Sun bone houses."

"You'll be paid handsomely," said Isidro. "Four sunstones, just for you." At first he smiled, but the smile faded into a grimace, transforming his sun-scorched face into a mass of wrinkles.

He looked hard at Alec. "That's what you care about most—money—isn't it?"

Alec shook his head in protest, but Isidro's words stung. Only minutes ago, he had been staring at a dead man's bracelet and congratulating himself for landing the furriers. He had been so swept up in the glory of it all that he had forgotten that Isidro was here to mourn his daughter and grandson.

That was the problem with Edgeland. You got so used to death, so used to all the dead bodies—everywhere—that sometimes you stopped seeing them. Stopped feeling for them. Sami Aron was like that. Sometimes Alec was, too.

"It's all right," said Isidro finally, with a shake of his head. "I was the same way when I was younger. I dragged my daughter and grandson to the Far North in search of these stones. And look what it got me." He glanced back to their frozen bodies. "It makes you wonder whether you can *really* take anything with you . . ."

"We will take care of you and your dead," said Alec. "House Aron is truly the best at preparing the dead for all the pleasures to come in the afterlife."

"I want to be prepared," said Isidro. "But we have what matters most: my family and precious jewels. When I get out of purgatory, I want them with me."

"Yes," said Alec. "And soon all of you will be in the Sunlit Glade . . ."

Isidro waited for him to continue speaking. Alec knew what to say. "And when you walk together, on the mossy carpet of the Sunlit Glade, you'll be at peace."

"At peace," repeated Isidro. He looked at Alec thoughtfully. "You can get the amulets?" His eyes flicked back to the frozen corpses.

"Yes," replied Alec. "I believe so."

"And the poison," said Isidro.

"Are you sure—" began Alec.

"Yes!" snapped Isidro, eyes suddenly furious.

Alec fidgeted uncomfortably under Isidro's gaze and eventually nodded.

"Remember the poison," said Isidro, clapping Alec on the shoulders. "Strong enough to kill a tough old sea captain like me."

# CHAPTER 8

Sometime later, Alec left House Aron and hurried back toward the pier. It was dusk now, and the sky was turning purple. If everything went right, there would be just enough time to launch the funeral scows before dark, about three hours away.

The streets were filled with Suns doing last-minute errands in preparation for night. During the long hours of dusk—and dawn—the Rule of Light allowed the Suns and Shadows to be in the same areas, although they still avoided each other.

Shadow vendors were already entering the streets to set up their exotic wares: jars of fireflies, mummified bats, owl feathers, scented mushrooms, and brightly painted papier-mâché skulls.

"A dirty lil' grayling butchered ol' Freddy in plain view," a potbellied mushroom seller was telling a woman, his hands slashing at the air in front of him for effect. "But you can bet that a Sun put th' grayling up to it. Them Suns'll pay for this, they will. If that grayling ain't found by dawn—blood will run in the streets. *Sun* blood. Mark my words, if . . ."

The mushroom seller paused to look around. Alec sped toward House Aron's pier. Again he read the note that Ellie had passed to him only minutes ago: *Meet me at your pier. Urgent.* It wasn't signed, but it was Wren's handwriting.

House Aron dockworkers were out in full force across the length of the pier, preparing scows for Isidro's funeral. Alec spotted Wren standing behind a nearby fisherman's shack at the edge of the pier. She was wearing her wig and her reversible robe. To his great relief, Wren didn't look hurt.

"Well done with the furriers," she said as he approached. "Your house must be swimming in sunstones." She rubbed her thumb and forefinger to indicate the vast sum of money.

Alec grinned. "You should have *seen* me out in the water—it was . . ." He was about to continue talking, but he noticed that Wren was shifting from foot to foot as he spoke. And her forehead was creased with lines.

"Enough about the furriers," he said. "What happened? What's so urgent?"

She looked awkwardly down at her feet. "I hit my goal. I'm leaving soon. On a ship. *Really* soon."

"Oh," said Alec. He swayed backward, though his feet were rooted to the spot. "That's good. I mean, good for you."

"Yes," said Wren. She glanced off at the distant dockworkers. Anything, apparently, was better than looking at him. "It's good. I leave just before sunrise."

Alec sucked in air through his teeth. He'd always known that she wanted to leave, and he agreed that she *should* leave. But her actually going was a different story. Wren was the closest

44

thing he had to family on Edgeland, maybe even anywhere.

"Edgeland will be strange without you," Alec said, scuffing his sandal back and forth over the splintery wood of the pier. "I'll never forget the way you were when we first came here. You helped me so much."

"If you say so," said Wren. Her mouth cracked into a little smile.

Alec smiled too. "You were really nice to me. Well, most of the time, anyway. You were the only person who bothered to come into my room when I had those nightmares. Where did you even learn to sing like that?"

"My dad taught me those songs," Wren said. For a moment, Wren's eyes glazed over. "Maybe I'll learn a few more like that—if I can ever, you know, find him."

Alec swallowed hard and nodded.

"I hope so," he said. "Do you have a plan yet for how you're going to find him? I mean, a plan is important. Maybe you want to stay for a few more days to . . ."

Wren shook her head. "Alec, it's no good for me here," said Wren. "I never felt right at House Aron . . . And now . . . I'm sort of in trouble."

"What kind of trouble?" Alec asked.

"People are looking for me," said Wren. She shifted her eyes from left to right, scanning her surroundings, as if her pursuers might be standing nearby.

"What people?" he asked.

"Listen—I didn't actually *do* anything," said Wren. "I was just walking when—"

A high-pitched scream interrupted their conversation, followed by a plume of smoke rising into the air. Then another scream. Wren and Alec ran toward the sound. Smoke poured out of a descender jutting from the shoreline near House Aron's pier, and a small grayling—perhaps a five-year-old—lay on the ground beside it. His hands and arms were bleeding, and his face was an unnaturally bright red. Blackened clothes stuck to his body.

Wren fell to her knees and gingerly put a hand on his chest. The boy shrieked. Wren snatched her hand back and looked at Alec as the boy began to whimper.

Alec knelt next to Wren. Glistening red blisters were forming across the boy's face and arms. He was still but for his eyes, which moved wildly in their sockets.

"What happened?" Wren said. "Can you speak?"

"They set a fire," he whispered. His throat bulged with the effort to speak. "Our rat hole got burned up . . ."

Smoke continued to billow from the descenders. Alec lifted the boy, who gasped, then went limp. With Wren's help, Alec moved him away from the pipe as quickly as he could, and then set him down on the ground. He was about to run for help, but the boy began writhing. A second or two later, his body went still.

He was gone.

Wren gasped and fell to her knees.

Alec kneeled next to the boy. Immediately, he murmured the Sun Prayer to the Newly Dead and closed the boy's eyelids. He looked at Wren, nodded somberly, and lifted the boy. Then he started walking away.

"Where are you taking him?" Wren called out.

"House Aron," Alec replied, his voice dull and wooden.

Wren watched as Alec walked into the street. Several Shadow peddlers stared, but no one stood in his way. It occurred to him later that he hadn't even said good-bye to Wren.

# CHAPTER 9

Wren watched Alec until he disappeared. She glanced back at the descender that killed the boy and realized suddenly what this meant for her. An instant later, she was running toward the Shakes. The descenders she passed were all billowing plumes of black smoke. *They're burning—the descenders are burning.* There was plenty of rubbish down there—rubbish that could fuel a fire. It was probably the Shadows—trying to smoke out the graylings. Trying to smoke *her* out.

Wren could only think of one thing. *My stash. The dinar.* It was still in her hole. In her hiding place. She had debated whether it was safer there, or in her pocket, and decided to leave it behind when she visited Alec. *Idiot! What was I thinking?*

Wren took the Corkscrew—a twisty road that ran the length of the island. A great many Suns lived here, and this close to sundown, it would be largely empty. She slowed down, out of breath, and considered the body-washer clothes she was wearing under her usual cloak. These suited her in normal circumstances, but if they were looking to hang a grayling for Fat Freddy's death, her usual disguise might not disguise her well enough.

Descenders all along the Corkscrew belched black smoke, and dozens of long, oily-looking snakes slithered out of them, coiling around one another in a frenzy to reach the surface. Apparently, the graylings weren't the only ones trying to escape their underground homes.

Wren raced onward and continued down the Corkscrew until she reached the turnoff that led to the Shakes. A few vendors stood idly by their stalls, staring at the foul-smelling marsh. Wren followed their gaze toward a column of black smoke rising from the other side of the Shakes. Her heart sunk. *Irv's place.* She sprinted toward the fire. A small throng of people were gathered around a burning hut.

Wren elbowed people aside, hiding her face to protect it from the heat. Sparks spiraled in the air around her. She made her way to the side of the hut, where she found Irv, covered in soot and sitting in the damp mud of the marsh.

Wren fell to her knees next to him. "Irv!" she shouted. "*Irv!* What happened? Can I get into my descender?"

Tears welled up in the old man's eyes. "It-it was . . . the . . . lamp oil," he said. "Heat from the other descenders. The bottles . . . exploded, then the fire came up the tunnel and torched my place." He looked at his gnarled, reddened hands and began to weep.

Wren looked at the shack. It was beyond saving.

Irv rose slowly to his feet. Wren tried to help him, but he shrugged her off. "You gotta go," said Irv. His voice sounded hoarse and dry. "I'm fine . . . but you gotta leave. They're really serious this time. Back in the Shakes, I seen a bunch of Shadows grabbin' graylings as they came out of the descenders. They're on the hunt. And it's gonna get worse when the night comes. Th' Shadows are out for blood." Irv gasped for a breath of air. "Wren, you gotta hide. I don't know where, but . . ." He wiped the tears from his face. "I'm sorry about the descender. Maybe it'll be okay to come back in a few weeks."

Wren nodded, forcing herself to remain calm. She pulled up her hood and began walking away, along the edge of the marsh. The sun was a thin slice jutting out from the horizon. She had nowhere to go. And nothing to her name. Her stash was gone. Burnt up. Nothing could've survived the heat of that blaze.

The foul smell of the marsh was getting stronger. Wren walked faster, trying to find fresh air. She replayed the events leading up to Freddy's death. Several people had gotten a good look at her face, including Dorman. Sooner or later, someone would identify her. *This is really bad.* Suddenly, she bent over and vomited. Afterward, she spit repeatedly, but the bitter taste lingered in her mouth.

*Who will help me?*

Moments later, Wren was running again—back toward the place that had banished her.

Back to House Aron.

# CHAPTER 10

An enormous portrait of Ember Aron dominated the chapel on House Aron's top floor. Ember had long white hair, piercing blue eyes, and an utterly serene expression. Her face flickered with a rainbow of light created by stained-glass windows that surrounded the portrait. Combined with the glow of the sunset, the effect was enough to turn the most fervent nonbeliever devout.

The colors played across Alec's face, too, as he knelt in front of the wooden coffin that held the boy's body. *The boy.* That's how Alec had referred to him when he ordered the servants to prepare his funeral. "Who will pay for this *grayling*?" one servant had asked. "House Aron," said Alec, with as much authority as he could muster.

Alec gazed up at the image of Ember Aron. *You're happy that I'm doing this—aren't you?* Ember was renowned for her kindness and wisdom. Some even called her a prophet because she had visions of what the Sunlit Glade looked like, what it smelled like, what it felt like.

Alec looked down at the coffin and shivered. *This could have been Wren.* Alec had been in the descenders only once and was horrified by the filth and darkness, and the strange creaks and groans that came from the pipes. Having seen his reaction, Wren never asked him back. And to think that Wren had once been an apprentice like him. The other apprentices wouldn't be caught dead with a grayling. "Why do you still spend time with *Wren*?" Ellie once asked, crinkling her nose as if the mere mention of Wren's name might conjure the stink of the descenders. The last few years had been really bad for Wren, and Alec felt responsible because, well . . . he was partially to blame.

Alec looked down again at the boy in the coffin and closed the rough-hewn pine lid with the palms of his hands. "May your time in purgatory be short," whispered Alec.

Just then, he heard Ellie calling for him.

Alec left the chapel and met Ellie in the hallway. She ran toward him, her pale cheeks flushed red.

"Alec!" she panted. "Thank goodness I found you."

"What is it?" he asked impatiently.

"It's Isidro," sputtered Ellie. "He's at the pier . . . He's gone mad—touched with the death fever. It started when the descenders began smoking. He's screaming that it's the end of the world."

Alec closed his eyes in dismay. "Has he been given his last drink?"

"Last drink?" asked Ellie.

"His poison," said Alec, his voice rising. "Because if he has, it's too early."

Ellie wrung her hands. "I don't know, Alec—I'm sorry!"

"Come on," he said, adjusting his cloak. "Let's go see."

They ran down the stairs and out the back door of House Aron. Alec glanced about nervously, looking for signs of trouble. Fortunately, the narrow alleyway leading to their pier was nearly deserted. In the distance, however, they heard someone yell, "I saw two graylings over there!" Seconds later, someone else shouted, "Get them!"

"What if they think I'm a grayling?" said Ellie. She looked at him with pleading eyes.

"They won't," said Alec. "Look at your clothes . . . at the way you talk, and the way you carry yourself."

And it was true. Unlike Wren, Ellie looked like she came from a respectable bone house—and she always had—from the day she arrived at House Aron.

Together, Alec and Ellie raced down the alleyway.

At the pier they encountered Butros holding up his flintlock horse pistol as a warning to any would-be troublemakers. Next to him stood two of his men, each holding a musket. Recognizing Alec and Ellie, the guards stepped aside.

A whistle pierced the air.

Alec turned around and saw a young Shadow girl standing nearby, next to a pile of rocks along the shore. It was Wren, dressed in her reversible cloak, with the hood pulled over her head.

"Hold on," he said.

"But we've got to—" began Ellie.

"Give me a minute," said Alec. He walked over to Wren, who had traces of soot on her arms and face. She was teetering, as if unsteady.

"I can't talk long," said Alec. "I have to—"

"My descender burned up," interrupted Wren. The words came fast and low. "My stash is probably destroyed."

"Your whole stash?" said Alec. His mouth gaped open. "You kept it all in one spot?"

"Yes, I guess I was *very* stupid," said Wren, kicking at the ground. "What does it matter? It's gone."

"You can't stand around like this—in the open," said Alec. "They're looking for the grayling who killed Fat Freddy . . ."

Wren's eyes were red and watery. "They're looking for *me*," she said. "They think *I* killed Fat Freddy."

Alec was dumbstruck. "You?" he said. "But you didn't—"

"*Of course not*," said Wren. Her lips trembled. "A couple Suns killed him. But I found his body right before Fat Freddy's followers showed up, and they think *I* did it."

"Oh my God," muttered Alec. He had guessed Wren was in trouble, but nothing this bad. "We need to get you on that ship."

"I've got no money—zero," said Wren. "Weren't you listening? My stash is *gone*."

Alec's parents had given him some money, but it wouldn't be enough. And besides, he kept it at the Suns' treasury, which would already be closed with sundown so near. But there was another option. A better option. The furriers' sunstones. Isidro had promised him four.

"I can get the money," said Alec. He glanced at the House Aron pier and then looked at Wren. "I'm due four sunstones. Run to our old spot in the cave. I'll meet you there in an hour."

54

Wren dashed off, taking a path along the shoreline, passing the same descender that had killed the little grayling. She gave it a wide berth and continued onward, clambering over the slippery rocks.

Alec returned to the pier, where Ellie was waiting for him.

"Who was that?" asked Ellie, head tilted ever so slightly.

"No one," said Alec.

"Was it Wren?"

"Keep your mouth shut," said Alec. His tone was like a lash. Ellie winced and took a step back.

"Not a word," said Alec. "Do you have the amulets?"

"Yes," said Ellie, grateful to speak of something else. "I found them and made sure they were exact copies." She gave Alec a small velvet bag.

Alec took the bag and headed to the end of the pier. Ellie trailed several steps behind.

House Aron had worked fast, and the scene was set for the furriers' send-off. A dozen or so dockhands—burly men dressed in gray overalls—worked on preparing the nine funeral scows. All of them except for Isidro's were House Aron scows, and while Isidro's was longer than the others, it would still fit through the Ramparts.

Alec walked alongside the boats. Each one held four blocks of ice. Some of the blocks had begun to melt, and Alec could see air bubbles creeping up along the limbs of the entombed. Iron chests laden with sunstones and gems lay nested in the hull of each ship.

Several Blind stood at attention nearby, ready to participate in the send-off ceremony.

Everything was exactly as it should be. Except for Isidro, who was standing at the edge of the pier, staring off to sea.

Sami Aron watched from several feet away.

"Lola, my love, where are you?" Isidro called to the waves. "Lola!"

Alec hurried to Sami Aron.

"He won't get in his scow," said Sami Aron, using his yellow rabbit cloak to wipe the sweat from his brow. "He keeps calling for Lola."

Alec nodded. "Lola was his daughter."

Sami nodded. "Perhaps I gave him his last drink too early."

Ordinarily, Sami Aron would not take such an active interest in a funeral, but this one paid more than others.

"I'll talk to him," said Alec.

Sami Aron nodded, happy to pass the problem to someone else.

Alec took a deep breath and turned to Isidro. *Be calm.* Someone in House Aron had put together the last drink—a fatal mixture of spirits and spring-harvested hemlock. It was supposed to take hold quickly, but was not meant to be fatal until the funeral scows were well on their way to the Drain. Alec hoped the drink had been properly made. He knew that those who took the drink often had visions. On rare occasions, they went mad.

Alec walked to the edge of the pier. He shooed away a few seagulls, then approached the old furrier. "Honored Furrier—Isidro," he said. "It's me, Alec—I've found what you asked for."

Isidro turned toward him and blinked heavily. "You have the amulets?"

Alec nodded.

Isidro's eyes were cloudy, as if already veiled with death.

"I have them," Alec said. "One for your daughter and one for your grandson." He forced himself to look into Isidro's watery eyes.

"Show me," said Isidro hoarsely. His cheeks began to twitch. Alec opened the velvet bag and handed the amulets to Isidro. Ellie had done well to find them so quickly. He glanced back and saw her standing a few feet away, her face white with worry. After this was over, he'd apologize for snapping at her.

Isidro cupped the three amulets in the palms of his thickly calloused hands.

"Thank you," said Isidro, whispering the words into his hands. "Now I need to say my mantras . . . Drown the Serpent of Fear . . . And I'll be . . ." He paused. "I'll be done." Tears began to roll down Isidro's cheeks. "I have been sick with

57

worry," he said. "This island is cursed. Smoke rising from the pipes. Children being hunted. None of it is right." He started to cough. Flecks of spittle gathered at the edges of his mouth.

Alec shut his eyes. He envisioned the boy lying in the coffin, but for a second, he saw Wren lying there instead of the boy.

"I can help," said Alec, placing a hand on his shoulder.

"No you can't!" snapped Isidro, shaking off Alec's hand. "You're just a boy. You think you know what you're doing because you got me two amulets and a vial of poison?"

Alec shook his head. "I meant that I could help you find your fearstone," said Alec finally. "You do want to throw it, right?"

For those who believed they were near death, the Common Book advised throwing a fearstone into the water. The stone, it was said, represented life's worries and dreads.

"Yes," said Isidro, scratching his beard and looking around. His anger seemed to cool. "Yes . . . my fearstone."

Alec pointed to a large, rectangular slab of rock that had been placed nearby, in preparation for this moment. Isidro picked it up and heaved it high into the air, then hurled it down, creating an enormous splash.

"Yes," muttered Isidro. "That was proper."

Alec lifted his arm. Isidro took it and allowed Alec to walk him to his scow. Alec could sense dozens of eyes on them, including those of Sami Aron and Ellie. He tried to ignore them, and remain focused on Isidro. He just had to keep the old furrier calm.

"The last drink," muttered Isidro, clamping Alec's arm with a vise-like grip. "I can feel it working . . . It's making me . . . muddled in the head."

"You're doing fine," said Alec.

Before Isidro climbed into the scow, he stopped and patted Alec on the arm. "Thank you," he said. "I've left an iron chest with a hundred stones for House Aron," said Isidro. "You earned it. I included four extra stones in a cloth sack marked for you . . . as promised."

Four sunstones, just for him.

He still couldn't believe it. Four sunstones was a small fortune.

But then he remembered something.

"Left it?" said Alec. "Left it where?"

"In the basement," said Isidro.

"Basement?"

Isidro nodded. The light in his eyes was fading quickly. "I tried to find you, but they said you were attending a boy's funeral . . . So I left it . . . Don't worry—it's all there."

Alec frowned. He was supposed to collect the payment himself, then transfer it to the vault. But he'd always assumed that Isidro would pay him *here*—on the pier. It had been careless of him, but there was nothing he could do until the furriers had been launched.

The scows creaked as they rubbed against the pier. Alec gripped Isidro's thick forearms. "Thank you," he said. "You are very generous."

Isidro stepped off the dock and into his scow. He teetered

down the length of the boat, stepping over various iron chests, past the slabs of ice, until he found his seat on the bow. Then he sat and closed his eyes.

Alec turned to the dockhands and nodded for them to untie the boats. As they set to work, Alec began to sing the words of "The Northman's Dirge."

> *Death chills the blood,*
> *Ice binds the limbs.*
> *The trees that built the boats*
> *Sink now to the depths.*
> *The ghost-child comes to take away your fear,*
> *To bless these lives*
> *That began*
> *In the mists*
> *And crags and whorls of ice shadow.*
> *May the Sun warm you*
> *So you may thaw in the world-after, and live again.*

It was not a hymn often heard in Edgeland, but its effect was immediate. Sami Aron stood behind Alec, tears in his eyes. Ellie dropped to her knees and recited the sunset prayer. Farther down the pier, even the watchmen—who had been standing at attention—set down their rifles and bowed their heads respectfully.

The first star emerged in the eastern sky. With its arrival, bells began to ring in spires and turrets across the island. The seventy-two-hour day was nearly over.

As soon as Alec finished singing, the dockhands pushed the boats into the water. The current took hold of them as they floated slowly away. House Aron's pier was on the sheltered side of the island—not the side facing the Drain. For this reason, the scows would have a longer journey before being swept over the falls.

Sami Aron stepped forward, a broad smile on his face.

Alec stopped him before he spoke. "There's a problem."

"Nonsense," said Sami Aron, shaking his head in disbelief. "The ceremony was wonderful!"

"Isidro left his payment in the basement," said Alec.

Sami Aron's face whitened. He pursed his lips. "Alec! You of all people—you should know we never send them off without confirmation of the payment. Run and secure it. And pray it's all there!"

Alec nodded and turned to go, but Sami Aron stopped him. "Go to my storage locker in the middle of the pier and take a Shadow cloak."

Alec's eyes widened.

"I know, I know," said Sami Aron, taking in Alec's expression. "It is a sin, but this business with Fat Freddy will get worse, I fear, and I don't want you harassed by Shadows. The rest of us will go back to House Aron together. No one will bother such a large group."

Alec hurried to get the Shadow cloak, and hid it under his arm until he'd exited the pier. He waited for the watchmen to look away before sliding the cloak across his shoulders.

He was back at House Aron within minutes.

Using his master key, he unlocked the back door, which opened directly to the rear staircase. He ran down the stone steps two at a time and entered the basement.

The room was cold.

And empty.

Alec raced along the perimeter, but there was nothing there. Sweat blossomed across his chest and back. He circled the room again, slowly and methodically.

"Alec, it was so beautiful!"

Alec looked up. Ellie was at the entrance, beaming.

"I cried—the way you sung those songs—it was so, so wonderful!" But then she looked at his face. "What's the matter?"

"Isidro said he left an iron chest *here*." He looked at her, panicked. "*Where is it?*"

Ellie's eyebrows narrowed in thought. Then her face lit up. "Yes, we realized it had been brought down here by mistake. It's all taken care of. One of the Blind brought it to the pier. We put it in Isidro's scow."

Alec gasped and took a step back. He almost lost his balance. "The chest that was here . . . in this basement . . . It's on Isidro's scow?"

Ellie's face fell, and she nodded.

"Ellie," he said, his voice cracking. "That was House Aron's payment. Our sunstones, our jewels—everything the furriers gave us—it's going over the Drain."

# CHAPTER
## 12

For several seconds Alec's mind went blank. And then he was charging up the stairs, leaving Ellie behind. He burst through the back door of House Aron and ran to a bend in the road overlooking the harbor.

There they were. The scows were a half mile offshore, bobbing up and down in the chop.

Alec felt pressure rising with his chest. He wanted to scream. That payment was everything. If it fell into the Drain . . . *When* it fell into the Drain, he'd be ruined. Alec drummed a clenched fist against his forehead—hard. He could think of only one person: Wren.

What would happen to her? They needed those sunstones to *save her life.*

Alec stared at the boats in the water, as if the intensity of his gaze could turn them around. Isidro's scow was in front. If he had a telescope, he could probably see the chest that should have been in House Aron's basement.

And then a crucial thought broke through his despair: Isidro was in the scow he had made. It was thirty feet, longer than the others. *Thirty feet*. The vents beneath the Ramparts were only twenty feet wide. If the boat were spun in the right direction, at the right time, it would be trapped in the vent. *Stuck*.

There might be a way to retrieve those sunstones after all. It would mean jumping into the boat, grabbing the chest, and getting out again. *How long would that take?* Less than a minute. Getting down to the right place would be hard, but not impossible. There were maintenance ladders all over the Ramparts. All they'd need was a long pole to spin the scow and jam it. And all the luck in the world.

He looked again at the funeral scows, bobbing in the current.

But was there enough time?

Alec sprinted down the road, toward the seashore and the cave. As he ran, he watched Isidro's little flotilla move slowly around the island and toward the Drain.

Soon, he approached the cave and called for Wren.

She was inside, crouched against the slick wall, but rose quickly when she saw him come in—with such hope in her eyes that Alec felt thoroughly miserable.

He paused, reluctant to speak. The cave felt clammy and disgusting, like it was sweating.

"Alec!" she said, her eyes boring into his. "What's wrong?"

It was too difficult to hold her gaze. He looked away. "There was a mistake," he said. "Our money is on Isidro's scow—and it's *gone*."

"What?" Wren whispered. "*How?*"

"Wren—listen. We can fix this," said Alec, quickly explaining his idea for recovering the chest at the Ramparts.

Wren looked out the mouth of the cave, toward the sea, and nodded several times. "It's worth a try. I have nothing left to lose." She rubbed her forehead, wiping away the sweat that had gathered there like dew. "I know the quickest way to the other side of the island. Let's go."

Seconds later, they'd left the cave and were scrambling over the rocks like alley cats. With Wren leading the way, they hurried past the great seaside warehouses of the Coffin District. Afterward, Wren turned inland and cut across the island on a stretch known as Mourners' Way. If you needed extra people to cry, wail, and tremble at a funeral, you came here to hire them. A few mourners were standing about, looking bereft and ready for employment.

Alec glanced at their somber, silver-streaked faces, their gleaming robes and their blessing staffs. He had never been down this road at the beginning of Night. He wondered whether they could tell he wasn't a Shadow—and sped up.

They soon arrived at a long stone pier that jutted into the sea. They had made it there faster than Alec had thought possible. His chest heaved with exertion, and a cramp stabbed at his stomach like a knife.

"Do you have any water?" he asked Wren.

She shook her head. Her mind was elsewhere. Alec followed her gaze to the end of the pier, where curling waves frothed and crashed. A rickety vessel was moored there—a schooner with peeling red paint.

"Wait here," said Wren.

"Where are you going?"

"I have to talk to Crown," she said. "I'll be back."

65

Wren dashed down to the schooner and climbed aboard, while Alec remained crouched on the rocks beside the pier. He glanced about, searching for signs of trouble—sentries or curious Shadows. But there was no one. *Come on, Wren. Be quick, be quick.*

He had to get those sunstones back. For himself, and House Aron, but most of all for Wren. He owed her. Alec thought back to the night when she'd been thrown out of House Aron. There'd been a hunt to find the person who'd stolen that diamond ring. Sami Aron was enraged, screaming and threatening people. He was a bear when he was angry. Sami had come to Alec's room, pounded on his door. "Wren's the thief, isn't she?" demanded Sami. "Confess, little whiff, or I'm sending you home with a note saying that you failed me. What would your parents say? It was Wren, wasn't it?" And then Alec nodded and sealed her fate. The memory of it still made Alec wince.

Less than five minutes later, Wren returned with Crown, who was wearing an oilskin rain slicker, heavy boots, and a knit cap—a man ready for a sea journey. Alec climbed back onto the pier. Crown nodded and smiled, revealing a mouth crowded with yellowing teeth.

"So this is your client?" asked Crown, eying Alec. "The boy with the sunstones?"

"They're not *on* him," interjected Wren. "It's like I said— they're stashed down by the Ramparts."

"Right," said Crown. "And you need a skiff to get down there."

"Yes," said Wren. "You give us a skiff, and then at sunrise— when you sail—all you need to do is pick us up at Needle Island."

66

She pointed to a small outcropping of rocks that extended from the Ramparts to the sea, large enough to hold a lighthouse and a small temple.

"And when you get us," said Wren, "we'll give you a sunstone."

"A sunstone!" said Alec. Wren had lost her mind. It was an exorbitant sum. Plus, she was promising a sunstone they didn't even have.

"Haven't you two discussed this yet?" asked Crown, pulling at his scraggly beard.

Wren said yes at the very instant that Alec said no.

Crown *tsk*ed, and glanced back toward the schooner. "I have to get this boat loaded for another job. Do we have a deal or not? I think a sunstone is a fair price for smuggling a grayling off Edgeland right about now—given what's going on—eh?" He looked meaningfully at Wren. "By the way," he said, "your wig is crooked."

Wren held his gaze, stony-faced, and adjusted the wig.

Alec drew his unfamiliar Shadow robe closer to his body to ward off the evening chill. "How do we know you'll be there?"

"*You* don't—but *she* does," said Crown, gesturing toward Wren. "I wouldn't leave her high and dry—especially not with a sunstone on the line."

Crown turned to Alec. "I'm assuming you know how to handle a small boat in rough seas?"

"Of course he does," snapped Wren. "He brought the furriers to Edgeland, didn't he? Now take us to our boat."

The boat wasn't worth a sunstone. It wasn't worth a wooden amulet.

They found it tied next to the schooner. It was old and cracked, with a worrisome pool of water at the bottom—but it floated, and they wouldn't be in it for long. They climbed in and shoved away from the pier.

Alec started rowing. "What now?" he asked Wren, who was sitting in the bow.

"It's a straight shot to Needle Island," said Wren. "Keep rowing and I'll tell you if you need to turn." The boat struggled in the waves, and the water at the bottom seemed to be rising already.

"You do realize—I have no idea what I'm doing," said Alec as he pulled on the skiff's oars. "Last time I was in a boat, it capsized and went over the Drain." Their boat was almost an exact replica of the one that he'd used to intercept the furriers—an irony that almost made him laugh.

"That doesn't matter now," said Wren. "You just need to

row." She scanned the ocean with a brass monoscope that Crown had given her. She was mildly surprised to discover that it worked.

Alec kept pulling. "Are we going the right way?" They were only two hundred feet from shore, but already he could feel the current pulling them toward the Drain.

"There they are," said Wren, ignoring Alec's question.

"Where?" asked Alec, with mounting frustration. He glanced around hastily, but could see little. Alec caught fleeting, blurry glimpses of the Edgeland skyline.

"They're moving fast," said Wren, still looking through the monoscope. She turned back to Alec. The roar of the Drain was getting louder, and she had to yell to be heard: "Bring us a little more to starboard."

Alec glanced over his shoulder, trying to get his bearings. Finally, he saw the Needle Island lighthouse, a squat structure made of salt-stained gray brick.

The current grew stronger. Alec stared at his knuckles, which were going white from gripping the oars so tightly. Blisters were already forming on the underside of his hands.

Whitecaps crashed around them, and waves spilled over the gunwales. The roar of the Drain grew louder. Wren took up the spare oar and paddled. Alec braced himself, wedging his sandals into the crevices where the ribs of the boat joined the hull.

Alec pulled on the oars with a grim monotony. His entire body ached and his chest heaved with exertion. This was much harder than rowing out to meet the furriers. The water was choppier, and he was trying to row faster. In fact, it was probably the hardest he'd *ever* pushed his body.

It took only a few minutes more to reach Needle Island. The waves whipped the boat so intensely against the rocks that the hull cracked and water rushed inside. Wren threw her spare oar onto the pebble-strewn shore. Alec was exhausted. At first, he just lifted his head and stared dully at the waves crashing around him. Wren lunged forward, grabbing him under the arms and yanking him out of the boat. She succeeded in pulling Alec ashore, but—in so doing—her wig fell into the water and was quickly whisked away, along with the remains of their skiff.

Alec barely noticed any of this. He was hunched over on the shore, panting violently and swallowing down a bitter metallic taste in his mouth.

"Alec," said Wren, tugging gently on his shoulder. "We have to go." He nodded.

Wren was clutching the spare oar in one hand and the monoscope in the other. Her eyes were brimming with excitement. *She's actually enjoying this. Unbelievable.*

"I need an oar, too," he said.

Wren pointed out to sea. "Everything's gone. This'll be enough." She stuck out her hand. Alec grabbed it and stood.

Together, they scurried across Needle Island, past the little gray lighthouse and to the island's far end, where a staircase connected it to the Ramparts. Wren and Alec raced up.

When they emerged onto the path atop the Ramparts, Alec was surprised to see so much water. The path was covered with puddles. He panicked. *Has the Drain flooded?* According to the history books, the Drain *did* flood every few centuries. It last happened about five hundred years ago. The stories of it overflowing used to give him nightmares. But then he realized he was being ridiculous. There may have been more mist and water than usual, but there was nothing actually coming out of the Drain. He had to calm down.

Wren stood next to Alec. She was scanning the seas with the monoscope.

She could see that the current was herding Isidro's scow and three others toward a nearby vent. The other scows were farther away, strung out like ragged lamps along a string.

Wren began to run down the Ramparts' path. A crowd of people in Shadow mourning robes were up ahead. It was almost dusk, so it wasn't all that strange to see Shadows, but why such a crowd? There were at least fifty people, maybe more. Faintly, above the roar of the waterfalls, Wren heard them chanting: "Friderik! Friderik! Friderik!"

Wren cursed bitterly—the way only a grayling *could* curse. These were Fat Freddy's devotees—mourning his death. They might have already pushed his body into the Drain.

She was furious at herself. She should have realized Freddy's followers might still be on the Ramparts. And she didn't even have a wig to disguise herself. But it was too late to worry about that now. Wren returned her focus to the sea, saw the furrier scows approaching, and tried to guess which vent they would enter. After a few moments, she spotted the likeliest one. It wasn't far from where the Shadows were, but thankfully, it wasn't right beneath where they were standing. A small stroke of luck.

Wren walked quickly toward the vent, head down. Alec followed several paces behind. By the time they reached the right place, Isidro's boat was approaching a chute of rapids leading to the vent. *Not much time now.* Wren peered over the edge of the railing and quickly found the ladder, a series of serpent-shaped metal rungs bolted to the outer wall of the Ramparts. They were so encrusted with sea salt that they were almost perfectly camouflaged.

Roughly thirty feet below, a lip of rock formed a walkway on the vent's perimeter, a mere five feet above the water line. Clutching the spare oar in her left hand, Wren nodded to Alec and slipped over the railing.

She began to climb down. It was a treacherous descent, especially because holding the oar meant she had only one free hand. She leaned in toward the stone wall of the Ramparts to keep herself from falling.

Alec watched her for a minute. At one point, he turned his focus away from Wren and out toward the Drain. What he saw turned his stomach. It was a vast chasm of mist, clouds, and swirling wind, accompanied by a roar that sounded like a million angry whispers. It was one thing to read about the Drain; it was another to be staring down into it.

*I can't do this,* Alec thought. He couldn't imagine climbing over the railing and starting down the ladder. He wanted to call out to Wren to turn back. By this point, she was about ten feet below where he stood.

Someone shouted. Alec looked up. One of the Shadows had left the group of mourners to walk toward them. He was a slightly built man. The others stopped chanting and turned to watch.

As the man approached, he looked curiously at Alec, who

was ignoring him, pretending to be an ordinary Shadow tourist. As he neared Alec, he peered over the railing and saw Wren.

The man began to shout in a mad, frenzied voice. "That was the killer," he shouted. "THAT WAS HER!"

He approached Alec, his eyes bulging. "Stop!" he shouted again, much closer now. "Dirty graylings!"

Alec recognized the man. It was Dorman, Freddy's most notorious follower. Whenever there was a fight on Edgeland between Suns and Shadows, it was a good bet that Dorman was involved.

*This is bad.*

Alec swung his legs over the railing and began descending the slippery metal rungs as quickly as he could. His hands kept slipping and he nearly fell several times, but he hung on. Farther down, he could see Wren's worried face looking up at him.

*Clang.*

The rungs of the ladder vibrated.

Alec looked up and gasped. Amazingly, Dorman was climbing down after them.

"I'm not a grayling!" shouted Alec.

"Alec!" shouted Wren. "What's happening?"

Alec tried to move down the treacherous rungs faster. He'd almost reached Wren when he caught a glimpse of movement overhead.

Dorman had slipped, and was dangling with one hand. His screams were swallowed by the roar of the falls.

Then he lost his grip and plummeted down past Alec and

Wren like a dart, his silver robe fluttering around his flailing arms. A half second later, he vanished into the Drain.

Alec stared at the spot where Dorman vanished, his mind and body frozen in shock. Then he saw Wren move from the ladder into the vent, where Isidro's scow would soon appear.

Alec closed his eyes and shuddered. He hugged the ladder. *Don't think about falling. Keep moving.* He forced himself to continue down until he reached the walkway. There was no sign of Wren. He followed the walkway around a bend and into the vent. Here the rumble of the falls was replaced with the echo of water rushing through the narrow passage. Wren was just up ahead, thirty feet down the walkway, oar at the ready.

Alec joined her just as Isidro's scow appeared. Wren crouched and pivoted toward the oncoming boat, gripping the oar as fiercely as a hunter about to strike. The boat surged forward. Wren rammed the oar savagely into the hull, forcing it to spin so it was perpendicular to the current.

Waves hammered the boat's side, jamming it into place. The boat blocked the vent perfectly, like a bone stuck in someone's throat. Whitecaps crashed over its gunwales, filling it with water.

"COME ON!" screamed Wren. She leapt off the walkway and onto the boat.

Alec hesitated, then broke into a run and sprang off the walkway—yelling wildly as he leapt over the bow and crashed into one of its built-in wooden benches. Alec clamored to his feet and shook out his arms.

Nothing broken.

There were several loud thumps. Two furrier scows had

piled behind the boat, which had started to tremble. Alec clutched the gunwales and made his way toward the stern, past the first block of ice. Alec glanced at it briefly. It was the one containing Isidro's daughter and grandson.

Alec crawled up alongside Wren. To his great surprise, Alec saw that this block of ice contained the man who Isidro had killed. The ice had begun to melt, and the man's right hand—cold, wet, and white—was sticking out, along with his diamond bracelet, which sparkled in the water vapor.

For a second, Alec considered taking the bracelet—Wren might need it. But he could hear Sami Aron's voice in his head, even louder: *We do not steal from the dead*.

Alec continued on, following Wren up the boat. There was the bench built into the hull, laden with three iron chests. *At last!* Wren was on one side of a chest, struggling to drag it forward. Alec clambered over to help her, and the two inched their way to the stern. They were close, and the other walkway—on the opposite side of the vent—was just five feet above them.

It was their way out.

The boat was shuddering violently now. Behind them, the current pushed one of the other scows up in the air and over Isidro's boat. Wren shouted, but her words were inaudible. Together they lifted the heavy chest. Alec maneuvered around a tangle of ropes at his feet and stumbled, losing his grip on the handle. Wren yelled and strained to hold her end. Alec popped back up and grabbed the handle he'd dropped. At that exact moment, the surging current and the weight of the other scows broke the hull.

An explosive cracking sound echoed in the vent as the front third of Isidro's boat snapped off. Both parts spun away from each other, caught by the torrent of water rushing toward the Drain. Alec and Wren screamed.

The water catapulted the broken scow out of the vent and over the precipice—sending Alec, Wren, the dead furriers, and a great many sunstones into the misty, endless vapors of the Drain.

# CHAPTER 14

When Wren finally regained her senses, she opened her mouth to breathe. But instead of air, salt water snaked down her throat. She kicked and flailed, then felt herself being drawn upward until, at last, she broke the surface of the water. Wren gagged, and water spewed from her mouth.

Then she opened her eyes.

She was floating near the base of a massive waterfall fringed by sheer cliffs. Geysers of spray shot in every direction. She craned her neck up, trying to see the sky, but couldn't. Seconds later, the current whisked her away from the waterfall and toward a haze of fog and clouds.

A thought bubbled up into her consciousness. *I'm at the bottom of the Drain.* Then another. *Am I alive?* Wren grabbed her forearm and twisted the skin savagely. The jolt of pain that ran up her arm brought a wave of relief.

"Alec?" she called.

Her voice sounded weak and scratchy. She took a breath and tried again.

"Alec!"

There was no answer.

The current carried her quickly away. The cliffs, the water-falls, and the great plumes of spray all receded into the fog. Now the only signs of land were great slabs of black stone whose tops jutted from the water like the heads of sleeping whales.

"Hello?" she called softly.

She saw a body floating nearby, within arm's reach. It was a young man, face up, with stringy brown hair covering his face like strands of seaweed. His eyes were vacant and lifeless. Wren squirmed away.

Not Alec.

Soon Wren saw other bodies—dozens of them—floating like timber, all drawn along by the current. She drifted past an enormous boulder surrounded by a small pebble beach. It was bigger than the other rocks she had seen—practically an island.

"ALEC!" she yelled.

She scanned the water but saw only limp corpses bobbing in the chop.

"ALEC!!!" she yelled again, louder. "If you can hear me, swim to the island!"

Seconds later, a child's voice called back to her.

"Shut your mouth! They're huntin' for breathers like you."

The sound of another voice was startling. Wren sank down in the water so that only the top half of her head was showing. She looked around for the child, but the mist made it impos-sible to see more than twenty or thirty feet in any direction.

"Hey!" called Wren. "Who are you?"

Silence—nothing but the fading roar of the Drain.

Then came the sound of the child's voice again. "Play dead until th' others wake up. If you don't get caught, we'll find you. *Trust me.*"

Wren tried to swim toward the voice, but the harder she pulled through the water, the more the current tugged her away. She watched helplessly as the island melded into the mist.

Wren's mind whirred: Going over the Drain meant she must be deep underground. *But if this was a cavern, where was the ceiling?* Above her was an unbroken cloud, neither bright nor dark. Another thought formed in her mind. *Is this purgatory?*

Just then, something splashed behind her.

Wren jerked her head around, but the mist was so thick that she could barely see a thing. There was another splash. Maybe it was Alec. Or that kid who'd told her to be quiet.

Then a figure emerged. It was a man, holding on to a long wooden plank with one arm and paddling with the other. He had a hawkish nose and a razor-thin beard.

Dorman.

But how?

They locked eyes.

Dorman stopped paddling.

"YOU!" yelled Dorman, his eyes bulging and his face red. He splashed toward Wren. He was still clutching the wooden plank fiercely, as if afraid to let go of it.

"DORMAN—*wait!*" shouted Wren.

The man seemed stunned to hear his own name, and

79

stopped swimming for a moment. He was three or four feet away now, within striking distance.

"Dorman," she said again. "I know what you think I did—but you're wrong."

His face contorted in rage. "*You grayling liar.* I saw you standing over his bloody body!"

"Listen to me," said Wren, her voice pleading and insistent. "I'm not just a grayling. I have a name. Wren. Wren Brell. And I swear, on the memory of my dead mother, I didn't kill Friderik."

"There was blood all over your robes!" he shouted. "Your shoes were covered with it."

With his free hand, Dorman reached for Wren, grabbing her arm. She fought him, but he pulled her closer, and then—a second later—swung at her. Dorman's blow glanced off the side of her head.

Wren dove deep into the water, swimming beneath the surface until she ran out of breath. When she popped back up, Dorman was ten feet away, slapping his arms frantically against the water. When he'd struck Wren, he'd lost his grip on the wooden plank, and now it was nowhere to be seen.

Suddenly, a skinny boy with hair braided close to the scalp appeared behind Dorman.

Alec.

Dorman didn't see him; he was too panicked, flailing his arms and legs, desperately trying to stay afloat. The water rose past his chin. He screamed.

"Take my arm!" Alec yelled.

Dorman spun around so he was facing Alec, but he

swallowed more water and began to gag. He thrashed for a moment longer, then his entire head disappeared below the surface. Alec dove toward Dorman and grabbed his arm, trying to pull him up. But Dorman was heavier than he appeared. He began to sink, dragging Alec down with him. Alec held on for a few seconds, until his eardrums were about to burst from the pressure. He yanked as hard as he could, but Dorman kept sinking. When he couldn't hold his breath any longer, Alec released his grip and surfaced. Wren peered underwater to see if she could catch a glimpse of him.

But he was gone.

"I tried to save him," Alec sputtered.

"I know," said Wren. As she caught her breath, Wren tried to process it all. *First Fat Freddy, now Dorman. Who next?*

A minute or so later, as they continued to tread water, Dorman's body resurfaced. Now, he floated like the other dead that surrounded them. His mouth was open and his eyes were two glassy orbs.

"Alec!" she gasped. "We have to get out of here!"

Alec looked at the mist, the calm water, and the floating bodies around them. His face was pale. "I wish we could," he said. "But I don't know where to go."

# CHAPTER 15

Alec was the first to spot the wooden raft.

It floated nearby, carrying the bodies of an elderly couple that were tied to it—and to each other—by a coil of frayed twine. It was an old Shadow tradition to bind a married couple in this manner when they died on the same day. Since it was considered unseemly for Suns to show interest in Shadow death rituals, Alec had never actually seen it done. He had only read about it.

The raft was made of a single slab of pine. That's probably how it survived the falls. The splintered remains of other rafts floated nearby, along with countless bodies—those of Suns *and* Shadows.

"Any idea where we are?" asked Alec as he turned toward Wren. She was treading water quietly, right alongside him.

"You'd know more than me," she said. "You're the one who reads all those books."

Alec didn't reply. Instead, he shivered. The adrenaline from the encounter with Dorman had begun to wear off, and he was starting to get cold. He pumped his legs under the water, trying to keep his blood flowing.

"Call me crazy," said Alec finally, "but I think we might be on the River of the Dead. It's what takes you to the Purgatory Isles."

"So much for meeting Crown at dawn," said Wren.

"You might just be the most unlucky person I know," said Alec. "No offense."

Wren started to shiver as well. She could feel the water sucking the heat from her body. She began swimming toward the married couple's raft.

"What arc you doing?" Alec asked.

"I need to get out of the water."

Alec looked at the raft, studying the old man and woman who were tied to it. "But they're Shadows," he protested.

She frowned at him. "So what? You think all those Edgeland rules apply down here? Well, I'm not standing on ceremony. Not anymore." She pulled herself onto the raft. "Come on," she said, gesturing for him to join her. "You're cold, too." She held out an arm. Alec took it and pulled himself up onto the raft. As he did this, he accidentally brushed the hand of the old woman. He was startled to feel that her skin was taut and almost warm.

"What is it?" asked Wren.

"Her skin . . . ," said Alec. "It's still warm. It's like . . . she *just* died."

"Don't touch her again," said Wren.

"Why not?" asked Alec.

Wren went on to tell him about the child's voice—the one

that had told her to play dead because they were hunting for "breathers."

"Who do you think the child was?" Alec asked.

"No idea," replied Wren. She shook her head and felt a rivulet of cold water trickle down her neck. "We should probably get back in the water," she said. "But I gotta warm up a bit first."

Wren looked around, trying to discern where they'd come from, but it all looked the same now—an unbroken expanse of water and fog. She thought she heard the faint rumble of the Drain, but it was so distant that she wondered if her ears were playing tricks on her.

"We need to get back to the Drain," said Wren. "When I came to, I could see a long ways up. On one side, near the waterfall, there were cliffs that looked climbable. It was hard to tell for sure, but if we had ropes, we might be able to—you know—make our way back."

"It'd be a crazy climb," said Alec.

"No crazier than anything else we've done," said Wren. "I mean, didn't we fall into the Drain and *live*?"

"I guess," Alec said, frowning. "But we'd need a boat."

"Look around," said Wren. She waved her hand at all the debris in the water, including a great many wooden planks. "We could build something if we had to."

Alec eased a little farther onto the raft, trying to get comfortable. "It still seems crazy," he said. "If this is the River of the Dead, and we're headed toward the Purgatory Isles, can we really just climb our way out?"

A sudden movement drew Alec's attention. What he saw

made him lurch forward, nearly toppling off the raft. It was the old woman next to him. The old, *dead* woman. Her hand was twitching—then jittering, faster and faster until her knuckles rapped against the wooden deck of the raft.

Wren gasped and slid away until she teetered on the very edge of the raft.

Alec had been around enough dead bodies to know that they sometimes spasmed. Fingers could twitch. *But like this?*

A second later, the woman sat up.

Alec grabbed Wren and pulled them both into the water. They quickly surfaced and discovered the old woman staring at them.

She blinked owlishly and licked her lips with a thick white tongue. "Jonas!" she rasped. "Where's my Jonas?" Her eyes darted about, and she rotated her neck until it cracked loudly. "Jonas!"

The old man next to her began to twist and squirm. "No need to shout, woman," he groaned. "I'm next to you." He struggled to sit. Stringy locks of hair hung over his face. He opened his mouth and yawned, revealing a set of crooked jack-o'-lantern teeth. "Guess we're still together."

"Thank the Shadow," said the old woman.

"Don't thank 'em yet," said the old man. "This ain't no moonlit beach, filled with food and drink and pretty people. We still got purgatory ahead of us, woman. I'll have to pretend to be good."

"Quit yer blasphemy, fool." The woman worked to loosen the twine that bound them. Suddenly, the twine snapped. The woman looked around as if searching for something she had misplaced. When she saw Alec and Wren floating in the water next to the raft, she nodded with satisfaction.

"There they are! Bless the dear Shade—we ain't the first to wake after passin' through th' Drain," she said. "These two are just cuddlin' together, sweet as can be." She eyed their silver robes. "How'd you die, little Shadows?"

The woman studied their faces, as if divining their stories. "Oh, I see . . . a sudden death. A lovers' quarrel turnt bad?"

Her husband frowned. "A lovers' quarrel," he said, in a voice so deep it sounded like it came from the bottom of a well. "Bad things come from a lovers' quarrel. But you'd know that now, wouldn't you?" he said to Alec.

Wren frowned. "We're not . . ."

The old man stood, causing the raft to tilt dangerously. "You've undone our ropes," he said. "Marjorie, why'd you do that?"

Marjorie pursed her lips. "I don't plan on stickin' around in purgatory for long," she said. "But you . . . with yer drinkin' and yellin' and startin' fights. You'll be there a while, Jonas. A good long while. Until you're *ready* for the Moonlit Beach."

"That ain't true!" yelled Jonas. "It's your fault we died! Or d'ya not remember that? I always said not to drive th' wagon so fast, but you're as stubborn as a mule and ya got us killed!"

They kept shouting at each other, ignoring Wren and Alec.

Wren watched them bicker for another few seconds.

Alec nodded toward the water.

They swam away from the raft. Soon they came upon the body of a middle-aged woman lying faceup in the water. Her neck was beginning to spasm, causing her head to wobble.

Alec and Wren swam away, but bumped into a teenage boy whose teeth were chattering so loudly that they sounded like a woodpecker hammering away at a tree. All around them, bodies were beginning to jitter and convulse.

Alec and Wren had nowhere to go. Finally, they stopped swimming and treaded water, their backs to each other, and stared mutely as the dead woke up.

# CHAPTER 16

All around them, people began to call out.

"Get off me!"

"Help!"

"Where are we?"

Then in the distance, as if answering these questions, came the sound of a girl, singing in a loud voice that cut through the discord:

> The town of Bliss leaves nothing to chance,
> They pack their bags and have a dance.
> The townsfolk leave when the sun goes down,
> The island's there, with no one around.
> I should take a peek at night, they say
> But the town of Bliss is far away.

As the voice drew closer, and became louder, everyone fell silent—mesmerized by the song. Then a canoe emerged from the mist. Sitting in it was a small grayling in tattered, ashen-colored robes.

"Let the river take you," chirped the grayling. She had a pinched face, with a thin nose and narrow eyes. "Be calm and follow the current. Purgatory awaits you."

Alec and Wren were both staring at the canoe.

"We could take it," whispered Wren. "We could knock her into the water. It'd be two on one."

"Then what?" asked Alec. "We have no ropes. How do we get up the cliffs?"

Wren was about to respond that they should try anyway, but four more graylings arrived, each in their own canoe. Some had traces of red in their hair, an indication that they'd once been child servants in the bone houses of Edgeland.

Wren waited and watched to see how people reacted. Would a mob of grown-ups really take orders from graylings? It certainly wouldn't happen on Edgeland. And yet there was something about how the graylings moved—as stealthily as the fog itself—that had a chilling and silencing effect.

"Did you see any breathers?" the grayling with the pinched face asked the ones who'd just arrived. They shook their heads. "Well, I'm gonna circle back—make sure we didn't miss any." She paddled into the mist.

Wren swam close to Alec, grabbed his shoulder, and whispered directly into his ear, "I think they're looking for *us*—we're the breathers."

Alec looked uncertain. "Should we say something?"

"No," Wren replied. "Let's do what we were told." She

glanced furtively at the dead around them. Now that they'd woken up, they didn't really look dead at all. In Edgeland, it was often hard to beautify or dress up a corpse—especially if their deaths had been physically traumatic, like being burned in a fire or falling from a roof. Here the dead all looked . . . rather well. Even Marjorie and Jonas—who had, apparently, died in a road accident—were undamaged. No gaping wounds or missing limbs. The process of awakening seemed to make the dead whole.

Gradually, the current whisked this sprawling flotilla, bodies and canoes alike, downstream. They drifted for many hours—though it was impossible to say exactly how long. After the initial panic, a dreamlike calm settled over everyone. They bobbed along placidly, like so many pieces of driftwood.

Eventually, an island appeared on the horizon. As they drew nearer, Wren and Alec could see docks jutting from the shores and buildings covering the landscape. The island's tallest and most prominent feature, however, was a massive stone wall that ran down its center and made the surrounding buildings look small.

"Where's the second island?" asked Alec. "There are supposed to be *two* Purgatory Isles."

Wren shrugged. She'd never studied the Common Book, but she knew the basics: The Purgatory Isles were where the dead stayed—for decades, centuries, even millennia—until they were ready to enter heaven. *So how many dead were here?*

While wiping her face, Wren noticed that her bracelet was gone. She looked up and down her arm, and then whirled around in the water, hoping to see it floating in front of her.

An awful, sinking feeling filled her stomach. Probably it had been ripped off during the fight with Dorman. Or maybe she'd lost it as she was catapulted into the Drain. In light of everything she'd been through, this hardly seemed like it should matter.

And yet it did.

The wooden carving was a physical connection with her mother. It tied her to the part of her life that had been good. Now it was gone; suddenly everything seemed lost. But then, ever so slowly, an idea began to form in Wren's mind. *Is my mother down here?* It was such a strange and unsettling notion that she stopped treading water and let her body descend for a moment.

When she resurfaced, she considered the possibility again.

She imagined meeting her mother, but quickly realized that Alinka might not even recognize her. The last time they'd seen each other, Wren was only eight years old. Wren remembered sitting in her mother's lap, at night, by the fire. Alinka used to love staring at the burning logs and telling Wren stories. In those moments, Wren remembered feeling safe. But had it really been like that? Or had Wren simply wished it to be true? Sometimes Wren thought her mother had become more of an imaginary friend than a real person from the past.

Reluctantly, Wren forced these thoughts out of her head. *Stay focused,* she told herself. *What matters now is returning to the Drain. And finding a way back up.*

# CHAPTER 17

Alec watched the island grow larger. What emerged was a monotone landscape covered with windowless stone buildings. But most of all, his attention was drawn to the enormous stone wall that bisected the island, running across it in an unbroken line that curved and squiggled. Near the island's center the wall seemed to bulge on both sides, like a snake with a mouse in its belly.

The graylings continued to circle about in their canoes, herding everyone into a small harbor, where wide steps led up out of the water. Alec was several inches taller than Wren, and his feet touched bottom first. He was mildly surprised to realize that the Drain hadn't torn off his sandals. He and Wren emerged sluggishly from the water and began to climb the stairs.

"You there—Shadow—what's your name?" croaked a voice.

Alec and Wren looked up, startled. An old man in a black robe had come down several steps and was now standing in front of them, with a pen and a small leather-bound book in his hands. He looked impossibly old. His skin was slack as a blanket on a bed that hadn't been made properly, and his eyes were almost entirely white—two small hard-boiled eggs with the faintest trace of pupils. A dozen other old men like him were arrayed across the width of the stairs, posing similar questions to other people emerging from the water.

"Full name, Shadow. Hurry now—there's other people behind you," said the man, waving his pen at Wren.

Wren was so caught off guard that she answered honestly. "Wren Brell."

He nodded. "The names of your parents?"

At this point, Wren considered lying, but it seemed pointless now that she'd told him who she really was.

"Isaac and Alinka," she replied.

"When did they pass?" asked the man.

"Mom died four years ago," replied Wren.

"Your father?"

Wren hesitated. "Still alive," she said.

The man wrote this information down. "Dead brothers or sisters?"

Wren shook her head. The man finished writing, then turned to Alec to pose the same questions. Alec answered him quickly and—having no skill at lying—he, too, replied honestly.

"That was stupid," said Wren as they continued walking up the stairs. "We should've made something up."

"I don't know," whispered Alec. "It seems like the least of our problems."

They paused at the top of the staircase and stared into a

large courtyard. A tall wooden fence—made of recycled funeral rafts—enclosed the space. Alec felt as though he were entering a cattle pen. Several urns, resting on tall pedestals, burned brightly within the courtyard. On the far side stood the great wall itself, looming over them. Directly below the wall, built into the wooden fence, were two closed doors. These were the only two exits from the courtyard—and each led to a different side of the wall.

Nearly a hundred graylings stood along the courtyard's perimeter, their eyes as glassy as paperweights. One of them, standing nearby, fidgeted with something beneath his tattered robe. In the dim light, Alec saw a glint of polished metal. *He's holding a knife. Do they all have knives?* Alec quickly looked away.

They shuffled into the center of the courtyard and stood close to one of the urns, enjoying its heat. At first, there were only a few people around them, but gradually others arrived, filling the space.

"It was the wine," rasped a young woman nearby. A tattered Sun robe was plastered to her body, covering a dripping bridal gown.

An older woman, wrapped in a waterlogged woolen shawl, shook her head mournfully. "I think you're right—he poisoned us for the dowry, my dear."

"But why're Suns and Shadows mixed together?" asked the bride, her voice quavering. "The Common Book says there are *two* islands."

"Hush now," said the mother. "I'm sure everything will

be sorted out soon." She closed her eyes and uttered a silent, fervent prayer. "We need to trust in the Sun."

The last person to leave the water was an old woman with a severely curved back. She climbed the stairs slowly, wobbling along like a tortoise. When she finally joined the crowd, the graylings formed a line at the top of the stairs, effectively sealing off the courtyard.

Then the graylings began to chant.

Their high-pitched voices rang out like a children's choir:

*Shadows to the left! Suns to the right!*

*Shadows to the left! Suns to the right!*

"What's going on here?" a man called out, his voice rising harshly above the chanting. He was in the middle of the crowd, near Wren and Alec, waving his hand to get attention. "Why are *graylings* telling us what to do?"

Others began to protest as well.

As if on cue, the two doors by the wall swung open.

A man's voice rang out: "*Silence!*"

Wren moved to get a better look at the speaker. She caught a glimpse of a tall man, clad in silver robes, walking through the doorway on the left. At the same time, a woman in a shimmering gold robe emerged from the one on the right. Wren stood on her tiptoes so she could see them both.

The crowd went silent.

The woman smiled in a way that lit up her eyes, while the man's lips were pursed, his square jaw clenched with angry determination.

Alec gawked at the woman. He was astonished. He was

95

staring at *Ember Aron*. She looked exactly like her portrait in the house's chapel—from the blue eyes to the high cheekbones and narrow face. She'd died five hundred years ago, but here she was, standing in front of them. Alec suddenly felt a flicker of hope. Ember Aron was famous for her generosity and piety. If she was in charge, well . . . maybe things weren't so bad.

"That's Ember Aron," Alec whispered to Wren.

Wren didn't seem impressed. "I know," she said. "And the man standing next to her is Shade—the Shadow prophet. Irv was crazy about him."

Wren tapped Alec on the shoulder.

"I'm more worried about *him*," she whispered, nodding behind her. "He's about a hundred feet behind us."

Alec began to turn, but Wren grabbed him. "Don't look— or he'll see you."

"Who?" whispered Alec.

"Dorman—he's standing at the back of the courtyard. He'll go crazy if he sees us. And I don't think we want that."

# CHAPTER 18

Wren stood perfectly still, taking shallow breaths through her nose. There were a lot of people in the courtyard—at least several hundred—but it was only a matter of time before Dorman noticed them.

And then what?

For the time being, however, everybody's eyes were on Ember and Shade. Ember walked into the center of the courtyard, moving with the grace and fluidity of a dancer. Those nearby shrank back, as if frightened they might be too close. Two graylings trailed behind Ember, their eyes darting suspiciously around the crowd. When they caught up to her, Ember placed a hand on each of their shoulders.

Shade stepped forward and joined Ember, his silver-ribboned robe undulating like streams of rain on a summer afternoon. He, too, was flanked by two graylings.

"Where are we?" called a teenage girl, standing next to her mother. Her eyes were wide as saucers.

Ember smiled, flashing two rows of gleaming white teeth.

"You're *just* where you're supposed to be," she replied. "On heaven's doorstep."

For a moment, people looked around, as if checking to see whether they'd missed something. "This is Purgatory," said Shade, in a rich baritone that echoed across the courtyard. "And, yes . . . it looks like one island, but because of this magnificent wall, it's really *two*. One side for Suns and the other for Shadows."

Several feet away, the mother of the bride tugged knowingly on her daughter's arm. She had a look of profound relief on her face.

Ember continued. "Shade and I are the High Keepers. And we're here to make sure that each of you ends up on the right side of this most holy wall." She waved a slim arm at the stone wall that loomed over them.

The wall itself was smooth and covered with intricate geometric designs. Farther up, Alec and Wren could see carvings that looked like the meandering branches of trees.

Shade raised both hands, palms out, as if bestowing blessings. "As our graylings told you: All of you need to form two lines. *Shadows to the left. Suns to the right*."

Earlier, when the graylings had given the order, almost no one complied. But now the crowd fell into two orderly lines. There were no more questions, and people seemed relieved to have been given direction by two adults.

Alec and Wren joined the Shadow line. They had little choice. Alec was still wearing the Shadow cloak from Sami's locker, and Wren was wearing her reversible cloak—silver side out.

Somewhere in the back of the line was Dorman.

A half-dozen graylings carried out a small wooden platform and placed it next to Shade and Ember. The two High Keepers climbed onto it as they watched the lines forming.

"Excuse me!" called an elderly man who stood just ahead of Alec and Wren. It was Jonas—from the raft. At his side was his wife, Marjorie. "Your blessings—Shade? Beggin' your pardon, Prophet, but I'm wonderin' how long I'll be here. You see, on account of my wife bein' such a good person—bless her soul—she was afraid that we might be separated, if I had to stay here a long while. And it'd be awful hard on her." Marjorie shook her head in dismay, but said nothing.

"A very good question, proud Shadow," answered Shade.

Jonas nodded with satisfaction and nudged Marjorie.

"The answer is simple," continued Shade. "We've built a collection of bliss houses on both sides of the wall, where you'll sit and say your mantras. This is the key to entering heaven. This is how you *earn* your passage. And as you repeat these holy words, you'll fall into a kind of sleep . . . we call it bliss. You'll be quite content, why"—and here Shade paused to laugh—"some say that our bliss houses are *heavenly*. Shadows, your bliss houses will look like the Moonlit Beach. Suns, yours will look like the Sunlit Glade." He smiled at Jonas. "And trust me"—again, there was that rich laugh—"when you do finally make it to heaven *itself*, your wife will be so divinely happy there, she won't even notice if you're late—by a few days, or even a few years."

Ember clasped her hands together, as if in prayer, and then

flashed her dazzling smile again. "My dears," she said. "We've already started accounting for who is here, but before you enter your new homes, we'd like to ask you to help us check for breathers."

Breathers.

Wren slouched downward, as if she could shrink herself into nothing.

"Sometimes the living fall into the Drain," continued Ember. "We call them breathers, and they're not meant to be here. We need to find them so we can help them, too."

A murmur spread through the crowd.

"This won't take long," said Ember. "I want everyone to find a partner—someone you do *not* know—and take hold of their wrists. Then feel for a pulse."

Whispers rose from the crowd. Wren looked for an escape route. But there was none. Half a dozen graylings stood in front of each of the two exits. Wren turned to Alec. He was staring intently at Ember and his look was so . . . eager. Wren grimaced. She had a suspicion about what was going through Alec's mind: He wanted to *talk* with this woman. Wren gave his arm a hard squeeze and shook her head.

*Not now,* she mouthed.

Seconds later, a teenage girl with a long ponytail stepped toward Alec and reached for his wrist.

Wren was quicker; she grabbed Alec's arm and yanked him away.

"Find your own partner," hissed Wren. The girl frowned at Wren, but stepped away to look for someone else.

"Thanks," whispered Alec. He looked shaken. "I didn't even see her."

They clutched each other's wrists fiercely and drew close to one another. All around them, people were doing the same thing.

"Does anyone feel a pulse?" Ember called out. "If you can, I want you to call out—good and loud."

Alec and Wren could feel the other's pulse racing. They stood there, gripping each other's wrists, eyes locked, for what felt like forever. At last, Shade brought the exercise to an end.

"Thank you for your fine work," said Shade.

Wren eased her viselike grip.

"*No!*" screamed a man's voice. "I'm telling you—it ain't fine."

Wren's entire body stiffened. It was Dorman.

"I saw two breathers!" he yelled. "They were climbing on the Ramparts and then I saw 'em later at the bottom of the Drain, way before all the dead woke up. Right at the waterfall! I was alive, just like them. We fought—they stole my wooden plank and drowned me. But I bet they're still alive!" His deep voice echoed in the courtyard.

People began nudging and pushing to get a better view of Dorman. Then there was a collective gasp. Unable to resist, Wren turned and caught a glimpse of an urn falling off its pedestal. Sparks flew in a wide arc above the heads of several Shadows.

Immediately, people were jostling—pushing, shoving,

kicking. "It was the Suns who pushed it on us!" someone yelled. "I seen 'em!" Screams and shouts rang out.

"Silence—calm—all of you be calm!" bellowed Shade. "Graylings—restore order *now*!"

Along the perimeters of the courtyard, dozens of graylings scrambled forward in a flurry of motion, like crabs scurrying with the tide.

Wren and Alec hung on to each other and kept their heads down. In this chaos, someone tugged insistently on the bottom of Wren's cloak. She looked down. A grayling stood at her side—a small girl with an ugly raised scar that started near her eye and traveled across her freckled face.

"Let's go," whispered the grayling. "*Trust me.*"

# CHAPTER 19

Alec gaped at the girl. She had the pudgy cheeks of a child, but the eyes of an adult: stern and deadly serious. They were eyes that had seen things.

The girl kept a tight hold on Wren's cloak as she walked to the open doorway in the far-left corner—the doorway that Shade had used to enter the courtyard. Amidst all of the confusion and shoving, no one paid them any attention.

As they crossed through the open doorway, Alec slowed down for a moment, his mind suddenly flooded with doubts. He glanced backward, trying to catch a glimpse of Ember. If anyone could help them, surely it was her.

"Should we . . . ," began Alec.

But Wren and the grayling had already disappeared into a darkened, stone tunnel. Alec hurried to catch up with them. Several dozen paces later, the grayling stopped beneath a lantern hanging from the wall. She turned to face them. "I gotta go back now," she said. "Can't let Mother and Father know I was gone."

"You mean Shade and Ember?" asked Wren.

The girl nodded. "We're all one big happy family," she said, with a quick roll of her eyes. "Ain't that obvious?"

Wren placed a hand on the girl's shoulder, as if to keep her from running off. "Were you the girl who spoke to me back in the water?"

"Maybe," she replied, shaking off Wren's hand. "And maybe I was the one who knocked over that urn. But none of that matters right now." She reached into her robe and took out two tickets—of the sort used to board a ferry. She handed them to Wren. "The first number on the ticket is the address—you're in Bliss House Forty-Seven—and the second number is your seat." She gestured farther into the tunnel. In the distance, they could see another doorway. "It ain't far. Don't get close to anyone. You might cause problems."

With that, she turned and hurried back toward the court-yard. Wren and Alec needed no more encouragement. They walked quickly along and soon emerged from the tunnel onto a narrow, rectangular terrace made of polished cobblestones. On their right, the great wall loomed over them. Hulking stone buildings stood everywhere—drab, windowless blocks that resembled crypts.

The terrace was empty except for a lone figure—a middle-aged man whose bald head was peppered with flecks of seaweed. When he saw Alec and Wren, he waved excitedly.

"Excuse me," he said, hurrying toward them, wide-eyed and jittery. "Excuse me, but have you seen my daughter? The graylings—they took her away. I've been waiting here for her . . ." He glanced about again as if, perhaps, his daughter might have just emerged from some hiding place.

Distant sounds of shouting floated up from the courtyard. It was Shade, yelling at the top of his voice to separate into Sun and Shadow lines. The small riot had not yet ended. Still, it reminded Wren and Alec that people would start coming out of the tunnel before long.

Wren was about to pull Alec away from the bald man when a girl appeared on the other side of the terrace and approached them. She had a round face, framed by red hair that had been woven into a hood covering her head, neck, and back. Whoever she was, it seemed doubtful that she was the bald man's daughter.

The girl focused her attention on Alec and Wren.

"Welcome, honored dead," she said, in a monotone that hinted at her having uttered this phrase a thousand times in the past day or so. Silver bracelets around her ankles clinked and jingled. "Tickets?"

The man rose to his full height and bounced a bit on the balls of his feet. "Listen here, young lady," he said, chin high in the air, voice rising in indignation. "I come from the Eastern Crags, and I've been waiting here for my daughter. When will she be back?"

"I've told you already." The girl took a step forward, making her bracelets chime. "Your daughter's of grayling age. She'll be working for our High Keeper now, Shade." She frowned at the man. "Now get to your seat."

The man crossed his arms. "And if I refuse?"

The two of them locked eyes. It seemed as if the man might continue to argue, but an expression of weariness overcame him, and he did something most unexpected: He yawned.

"You're tired," said the grayling, nodding with satisfaction.

"Yes—yes I am," said the man slowly. "I'm *exhausted*." He began to massage his temples.

"It's the pull of bliss," said the grayling. "Go now. Go to your seat."

"To my seat," muttered the man. "But I . . ." After a moment's pause, he turned and shuffled off the terrace.

The red-haired grayling turned to Alec and Wren. "Tickets?"

Alec was so mystified by what he'd witnessed that he didn't even react to the girl's question. One second the bald man had been near hysterical, and the next second he'd *yawned*.

"Tickets?"

Wren nodded and presented the tickets that the freckle-faced grayling had given them.

"That way to Bliss House Forty-Seven," said the girl, pointing down a narrow alleyway that snaked between two stone buildings. "It's close."

They could still hear shouting from the harbor.

"Sounds like the Suns and Shadows are at it again," said the grayling in a bored tone. "Thank goodness for the wall." She raised her hand. "Go on now."

Alec and Wren set off, relieved to be on their own again. The alley was flanked by stone warehouses. The walls facing them were dotted with narrow ledges that held glass jars filled with small gray shards.

"What's with the jars?" whispered Wren, reaching out as if to grab one.

"Don't touch them," Alec whispered.

"What's in them?"

"Fingernail clippings."

"Yuck," whispered Wren, crinkling her nose. "Why?"

"Shadows say the fingernails of the dead are poisonous," said Alec, as if this were perfectly obvious. "They use them to ward off evil."

Wren glanced up and down the empty alleyway, then stopped and turned toward Alec.

"Alec, we need to get out of here—*now*," said Wren. "First of all, we're alive, and I want to *stay* that way. Second of all—I don't *care* if Suns and Shadows are separated—sitting in Bliss House Forty-Seven until we wake up in heaven does not sound like a good idea right now. Especially since we're not dead. And who put Shade and Ember in charge anyway?"

Alec's throat felt dry, and he swallowed once or twice before replying. Wren wasn't thinking this through. Ember was considered to be one of the wisest Suns ever to walk the streets of Edgeland, and Shade was equally revered among the Shadows. They *must* know what they're doing.

"I don't know who put them in charge, but how do *you* know what they're doing is wrong?" asked Alec. "This *is* purgatory, after all. It's not supposed to be a barrel of fun."

"Maybe," said Wren. "But something's wrong here. It feels like . . . a prison."

"We ought to talk to Ember," said Alec. "There must be a reason they're looking for breathers." He ran his hands over his braids. "She said they wanted to help. Maybe she could get us back up the Drain?"

Wren's mouth twisted into a frown. "I know you think

Ember is some kind of saint, but I do not think talking to her is a good idea. You heard what that grayling with the freckles said. They're *hunting* us."

Alec raised his eyebrows. "Sorry," he said. "But I'll take Ember Aron's word over some grayling we met a few minutes ago."

Wren reached into her pocket and pulled out the tickets to look at them again.

"Come on," she said. "Let's poke around this Bliss House Forty-Seven before we do anything else. Maybe we can find some rope or get a lead on a boat."

Alec looked doubtful. "What, we're just gonna stroll in there, and someone will give us a boat—*oh, and here is some rope too*—that's what you think?"

Wren shook her head. "No. We'll have to steal them. I have a lot of experience at that—ever since I was kicked out of House Aron." She looked at him pointedly.

Alec wasn't sure how to reply. Sometimes he wondered whether, somehow, she knew that he'd ratted her out. There was almost a hint of it in her eyes. Or was he simply being paranoid?

A flurry of bells began jingling—it sounded as though they were coming from a nearby alley.

Wren startled, then tugged on Alec's arm and started walking again. "Let's *not* find out what that's about."

Soon they came to a narrow stone entryway with a Forty-Seven carved above a wooden, barnacle-covered door. There was no knob—only a rope handle.

"Wait," whispered Alec, running his hand down the tiny

gap between the door and the wall. A cold, crypt-like air was seeping out of it. "Are you sure about this?"

Wren sighed. "Of course not," she said. "But we can't just roam the streets. By now Dorman probably told Shade and Ember everything. Soon the whole island will know there are two breathers on the loose." She paused, letting this possibility sink in. The jingling of bells was getting louder, and now they could hear the scuffling of footsteps. A lot of them.

Wren gestured toward the door.

"All right," said Alec.

Wren pushed the door open, and together they stepped into Bliss House Forty-Seven.

# CHAPTER 20

They stood inside the doorway, taking in the cavernous space. A single orb hung from the room's center, just bright enough to illuminate hundreds of ladders standing in rows, rising from the floor to the ceiling. Every ladder had wooden chairs attached to each rung. A person sat rigidly in each chair. There were people of all ages—from spindly grandparents to small children—and they were as still and lifeless as waxen figures.

Nothing moved.

Except for their mouths.

The lips of every last man, woman, and child in the room were in motion. Wren watched a little boy who sat on the bottommost rung of a nearby ladder. He was mouthing the same words again and again: *Drown the Serpent of Fear.*

Wren looked around at the others. "The mantra," whispered Wren. "They're all mouthing the mantra."

Alec nodded.

Together, they gawked at the scene before them. It was like watching a chorus of the dead, only it was utterly silent.

"Alec . . . Does the Common Book say anything about a place like this?" whispered Wren.

Alec leaned down to touch the gritty ground beneath his feet. It was stone covered by a few inches of sand. "I think this is supposed to be the Moonlit Beach."

"Yessssss," said a raspy voice that floated toward them through the darkness. "This is not the Moonlit Beach, but it reminds us of that heavenly place. There are hundreds of rooms like it in this bliss house. Course, we don't call them rooms. *Beaches* sounds nicer, don't ya think?"

Alec and Wren turned toward the voice. It belonged to an old man with stringy white hair, who sat on the lowest perch of a ladder about a dozen feet away.

"How did you die?" he asked, leaning forward conspiratorially. "Was it violent? Let me guess . . . The girl drowned and the boy tried to save her, then you both perished in cold northern waters. Am I right?"

"Yes," said Wren, lying with practiced ease. She sounded genuinely surprised. She and Alec hung back, reluctant to get any closer. "How'd you know?"

"It's common enough down here," said the man, with a dismissive wave of his hand. "Everyone who comes to the beaches in this bliss house hails from Edgeland and points north. Geography. That's how we sort our dead on this side of the island. Go next door, to Bliss House Forty-Eight, where they keep the Canyon Landers, and you'll find beaches and beaches filled with people who died of thirst."

The man eased out of his chair and walked over to a small torch hanging against the wall. He took it out of its holster, then hobbled toward Alec and Wren. When he was a foot or two away from them, he stopped and grinned. The whites of his eyes, lit up by the flickers of the torch, were a pale yellow, like the dog-eared pages of an old book.

"Those first steps out of the chair are always the hardest part," the old man said. His head tilted back at an odd angle, as if it weren't properly attached. "But I have to keep doing it—have to keep making that trip up to the Meadow—otherwise I'd be off in bliss. And I can't do that, as much as I would like to. No sir, I can't. Old Lamack's gotta look after his bliss house."

"Are all of these people . . . sleeping?" asked Wren.

"Sleeping is for the living, darlin'," replied Lamack. "You two and the rest of these folks are dead. Soon enough, once you sit in the chairs, you'll feel the pull of bliss—like a rock sinkin' to the bottom of the pond. Once you start yawning, there's no fightin' it."

*Yawning.* Wren glanced up at Alec, who nodded. That's what the bald man had done.

"And why'd you want to fight it?" continued Lamack. "It's bliss, after all." He cackled. "The fast road to heaven. You'll see, oh, you'll see. Now, where are your chairs?"

Lamack leaned in and took the tickets from Wren, then held them several inches from his nose.

"Well, aren't *you* the lucky dead." His mouth opened wide in surprise, revealing a few solitary teeth sticking out of purplish gums. "You got a spot on one of the nearby beaches. Bless your fortune! They're much nicer than the rooms—I mean, beaches—deeper below. How'd you manage that? Well, no matter. I haven't been on that beach in a while. I ought to look around—make sure all is well."

Lamack turned around slowly, as if his old joints were rusted tight, then began hobbling across the sand and deeper into the gloom of the vast space. Alec and Wren followed him, occasionally glancing up at the wax-like figures above them. One girl was clutching at her shirt, eyes opened only a crack, as if terrified of what she'd just seen. And there was a slender, willowy woman, hands clasped to her head, pulling at her own hair. Only their lips moved.

"These are the good seats," said Lamack, gesturing to the nearby ladders. "The folks here have been in bliss since before I came, and I showed up, well . . . a very long time ago. Couple hundred years at least. Been sayin' their mantras—waitin', waitin', waitin' for that sweet call to heaven. Should be soon now. Could be any moment. That's what Shade says. Gotta keep at it." He nodded and shifted his head back and forth, as if his words were music.

"Sir," said Alec. "How many people from this Bliss House have been called to heaven so far?"

Lamack ignored the question.

"Newcomers generally go to the lower beaches," he said. "I try to keep families together, of course. Got one family takin' up four ladders—beautiful family—all of them in bliss together, even the baby. All sayin' their mantras. Do you have any family that died recently?"

Wren hesitated. Her own mother would be tucked away in one of the island's many bliss houses—on the Sun side. Wren pictured herself back on the front porch of her cottage, where she'd grown up, sitting in that rocking chair. Then she pictured the women from the Sisterhood of the Sun: their old, wrinkly faces filled with sorrow. *Your mother is gone—you'll not see her again, child.*

"No family," said Wren, glancing at Alec.

"Me neither," said Alec.

"Well, sometimes that's for the best," said Lamack. "You don't age down here, of course. That can spook folks . . . Ah, here we are."

Lamack came to a halt. Before him was a darkened hole in the ground. Upon closer inspection, Wren and Alec saw that it was actually a stairwell. "Watch your step," said Lamack. "Ages ago I slipped and snapped a few bones in my neck. Didn't feel a blasted thing, of course, but as you can see, I'm all crooked now." He cackled again. "No matter, anyhow. Gives me a different perspective."

Lamack led the way down many flights of stairs. Every so often, there would be a doorway, but Lamack kept descending. Eventually, they heard a clanking from far below—the distant sound of metal striking rock.

"What's that sound?" asked Wren.

"Oh, that," said Lamack. "That's the diggers makin' more beaches—because, well, the dead keep comin'."

At one point, Lamack held his torch up to the wall, revealing the number 17 carved into the wall. "Good, good, good," he said. "This is your beach. Lucky you, moments away from bliss." He shuffled through a doorway, and they entered a large, echoey room that looked like the one where they'd first met Lamack.

They followed him between two rows of ladders, both full of people whose open eyes seemed to twinkle and glow in the light emanating from the moonlike orb overhead.

As they walked, they became aware of a noise up ahead.

"Oh dear," said Lamack. He quickened his pace until he reached an elderly woman sitting on the lowest rung of a ladder. She was whimpering and her shoulders trembled constantly. Lamack reached out and stroked her head. "Now, now, now," he said tenderly. "Easy, my love, easy."

"What's wrong with her?" asked Wren. She looked horrified. "Why isn't she in bliss?"

"Oh, she is—she is," replied Lamack. "For some folks, that's what bliss does to you. Most are real still—dead-like—but a few here, like this bitty, are always sobbin'—cryin' with joy, I'm sure." Lamack reached out to stroke the woman's head. "You're fine," he cooed. "Right where you belong, in peaceful purgatory. And old Lamack is here with you." Lamack continued to pat the lady's head and even began to hum a lullaby—as if she were a colicky baby.

Of all the strange things that Wren had seen since landing here, this was the worst. The old woman looked like a shopkeeper from the Shakes—with calloused hands and a withered face.

Wren stole a glance at Alec. His eyes were wide with shock.

The old woman's whimpers began to diminish, her shoulders relaxed, and at last, she stopped trembling. Once again, she was mouthing the mantras, just like everyone else. "See that," said Lamack. "It's almost like she can hear me. That's the funny thing about bliss—there are moments when folks seem to be coming out of it. But once you're in bliss, you don't come out. And this pretty lady, well, she'll be back to her sweet dreams soon enough."

Lamack smiled and shook his head, then shuffled onward into the darkness.

Alec could feel Wren's eyes, but he couldn't bring himself to look at her. Instead, he gazed up at the people in the chairs around him. He tried to imagine all the dead he had ever encountered at House Aron, sitting in Sun versions of these bliss houses—waiting and waiting. There had to be something good about this place, something he wasn't seeing. There had to be some reason why Ember Aron was involved. Alec had felt certain of this, but he could sense his certainty starting to crode, like a mound of sand crumbling at the water's edge.

Lamack led them across the room, past several dozen ladders jam-packed with bodies, until they came to one whose bottom two perches were vacant. "Easy-peasy. You're such lucky sods!"

A small brown-skinned girl in a stained summer dress occupied the third rung up from the ground. Her curly black hair was braided in pigtails that dangled to her elbows. Her mouth moved constantly, repeating the mantra like everyone else.

"Have a seat," urged Lamack.

Alec climbed up into the seat directly beneath the girl, while Wren took the one at ground level. Alec leaned against the back of the chair. He saw Lamack staring at him, so he closed his eyes, guessing that was what was expected of him.

"No, no, no," said Lamack as he looked at Alec. "Don't close your eyes. You ain't sleepin'. The trick is lettin' yourself be what you are. You're dead. Your body wants to be dead. So don't fight it! That's the key. You'll be in bliss soon enough. What you do is repeat the following mantra: *Drown the Serpent of Fear*. That way your lips keep mouthin' the words, even after your mind goes. Then you'll kind of feel yourself slippin' into bliss. After that, everything'll be fine. Here, look . . ."

Lamack swung his torch in a wide arc, stopping it just shy of a man's face. He was a strapping, muscle-bound laborer in well-worn coveralls. The heat of the flame blackened his chin. The man didn't even flinch.

"Don't!" yelled Wren.

"Stop that," said Alec. "Please."

Lamack laughed. "All right then, don't get all queasy. He's happy as a clam—on his way to heaven!" Lamack shook his head knowingly. "You new arrivals are all the same way, thinkin' the same kinda thoughts as when you were alive!" He waved his hand theatrically. "You're dead, so start actin' like it!"

Wren and Alec remained frozen in their seats. Lamack leaned in close to make a final point. His face was somber. "Now, just to be clear: Don't think about leavin' your seats," he whispered. "There are places not as nice as this. Got it?"

118

He patted them both on their shoulders, straightened up, and smiled. "I have to walk around, inspect the ladders, make sure all is well. Then I'll swing back. Check on you. Understand? But don't bother waitin'. You'll be too far gone to see me."

Lamack then pivoted and hobbled away into the gloom. Alec and Wren began to mouth the mantra, again and again. Their chairs were damp and cold, chilling them to the bone. Alec couldn't imagine how anyone could sit here, unblinking and unthinking. But then, of course, he wasn't dead.

Finally, he could wait no longer. He scooted to the edge of his chair and leaned down toward Wren.

"Wren!" he whispered.

She looked up.

"This is bad. We need to get out of here before Lamack comes back."

At that moment, a *tsk*ing sound floated down toward them.

Alec and Wren looked up, astonished. The little girl in the summer dress was leaning over the edge of her chair, her eyes open and alert. She was a wisp of a child—with spindly legs and a torso that bent toward them like the wilting stem of a dandelion.

"You're, w-well, you're . . . ," stammered Alec. "You're not in bliss." He looked around nervously, aware that his voice had carried farther than he expected.

"Fancy that," chirped the girl.

"Did you just get here?" asked Wren, straining her neck to look up at the girl.

"Nope—been here a very long time," the girl replied. "Stuck in this kid's body for hundreds of years." She frowned.

"Not what you'd call an ideal situation."

She moved sideways from her chair to the ladder and climbed down two rungs, so that she was almost eye level with Alec. "So, you got to meet Lamack? He's a real charmer." She reached toward Alec and ran a forefinger over one of his blond cornrows. He quickly pulled away. The little girl shrugged. "He's gonna be back here soon enough," she announced. "And then what'll you do?"

Alec and Wren exchanged glances. Wren was about to respond, but the girl continued to talk.

"Well, tell you what," she said. "Suppose I could help you?"

"We don't need help," said Wren. She crouched in her chair, ready to pull this girl away from Alec.

The girl stepped down another rung and again leaned toward Alec. He shrank back. "Oh, I think you do," she said. "Lamack'll be none too pleased when he finds the two of you—eyes wide-open—whispering to each other."

"We haven't really tried to get into bliss," said Wren. She got up out of her chair and stood at the base of the ladder, looking up at the girl.

"Well, you won't get into bliss, no matter how hard you try. You can't do it, because . . ." The girl paused and grinned. "Well, just because."

"Why aren't *you* in bliss?" Alec asked, eager to change the subject. "Aren't you worried Lamack will find you?"

"I can fool him and the graylings. I know my way around." She puffed up her chest and patted it with her hand, proudly. "I can be useful to you."

"Are you a grayling?" Wren asked. "You're the right age." She paused. "And you're awake."

Still on the ladder, the girl extended her right arm, as if about to bow. Her arms were even thinner than her legs, like two flimsy sticks wrapped tightly in brown skin. "I look the part," she said, "but I'm not a grayling. Not when I was alive, and not now." She held up her right arm. It was bent strangely at the elbow. "Shade doesn't use children who are broken."

Alec nodded and eyed the girl carefully. He had to figure out what was going on here. The freckle-faced girl had handed them a ticket, which led them to this seat, where this little girl was waiting for them. It might be a trap or it might be a rescue, but it certainly wasn't a coincidence.

"Tell me," he said, inching backward to put a little more distance between them. "Are all the world's dead on this island? I mean, hasn't anyone gone on to heaven?"

The girl raised her eyebrows. The effect widened her already-large eyes. "Nope," she said. "What you were told at the harbor is rubbish. I've been here longer than Lamack—'round about five centuries—and I've never seen *anyone* move on. Not a single person. That's the dirty little secret down here. Lamack knows it. The graylings know it. And Shade and Ember know it."

Alec leaned back in his chair. *Five centuries.* Alec imagined all of the clients who had passed through House Aron over the years. There must have been tens of thousands. And not one of them was in the Sunlit Glade. Could this be true? No. There was no way. And yet . . . what if it was true? Alec felt sick.

121

"I don't believe it," said Alec finally. "Purgatory is supposed to be, you know, temporary."

"Bring that up with the gods if you meet them," said the girl, twisting her mouth into a smirk. "But you won't find 'em here."

With that, the girl jumped gracefully from the ladder to the sand, about six feet below. "There's a way out of this bliss house—I can show you." She turned and started walking away.

"Wait!" said Wren.

The girl didn't stop. Wren and Alec jumped down from their seats and followed her.

"Hey—you! Where are you going?" said Wren.

"I have a name," said the girl, without turning around. "It's Flower."

Flower continued toward the far end of the room, past dozens of ladders stacked with people, until she reached a towering pile of broken ladders propped up against the wall. "Be careful here," said Flower. "Squeeze in slowly. It's tight for me and it'll be tighter for you."

Flower eased into a crevice between the ladders and the wall, while Alec had to push himself through rather forcefully, ripping his cloak and scraping his back as he went. It was easier for Wren. She was used to navigating spaces like these.

They emerged into a narrow space with an uneven stone floor. The only light filtered in from the hole in the wall they'd just pushed through.

"Where are we?" asked Alec.

"A staircase no one uses," said Flower.

Wren saw flickering lights far above. She sensed Alec standing next to her. "Are you sure no one else uses it?"

"Yup," said Flower. "These older bliss houses have tons of old tunnels and stairs that no one uses anymore."

Flower started to climb. The steps were big for her, and she had to use her hands to scramble up.

"Wait," said Wren. Flower turned around, her pigtails swishing back and forth like two rope swings.

"Before we come with you," said Wren, "I want to know *why* you're helping us. What's the catch? I mean, it's always something for something."

Flower ran her finger across her crooked arm, the one she'd broken. "Well," she said. "If you gotta know—I'm in need of a couple of breathers."

Wren's mouth opened, forming a tight little O.

"That's right," said Flower. Her voice grew deeper, suddenly sounding very much unlike a child. "I know what you are. And I've been waiting for you for a very long time."

CHAPTER
22

For a few seconds, the stairwell was absolutely silent, except for a distant *plip-plop* of dripping water.

"Why?" asked Wren. "What do you need breathers for?"

"I'll tell you if we keep moving," said Flower. "This is not a good place for a chat. Okay?"

Flower started again up the stairs. Alec and Wren followed close enough to hear her voice.

"You have a special ability—a power, I guess you could call it," said Flower. "You can revive people from bliss. You know, wake 'em up. All you gotta do is blow on them."

Wren closed her mouth abruptly. She exhaled through her nose, but still worried about the humid air escaping from her nostrils.

"Relax," said Flower, glancing back at her. "I'm already awake. Besides, you have to blow directly onto the face of someone in bliss. You didn't wake anyone up in that bliss house, did you?"

Alec and Wren shook their heads.

"I need you to wake someone up," Flower continued. "My friend Sebastian. He's on the Sun side of the island. If you do, I'll help you escape—get you a canoe, paddles, ropes, grappling hooks—everything you'll need to climb the Drain."

"You got it all figured out," said Wren.

"That's right," said Flower. "Like I said, I've been waiting for you for a long time."

"But will it work?" asked Alec. He rubbed his hands together as he climbed, trying to ward off the dank cold of the stairwell. "Can you really just . . . climb back up the Drain?"

"It's worked before," said Flower. "I got a breather out a few years ago. Climbed with her for hours, till we neared the top. Then we hit a layer of mist that I couldn't get through. She kept going. I know she got out—otherwise, alive or dead, she'd have floated back to this island."

As Wren groped her way up the stairs, she tried to picture it again—actually hoisting herself up out of the Drain on a rope, hand over hand. Maybe it was doable. But it sounded insanely hard.

"What do you think?" asked Alec. "I'm willing to try . . ." He started to cough. "My throat is really dry . . ." Wren slapped him vigorously on the back. She meant to help him, but she almost knocked him down

"Easy there," said Alec. "I can't climb the falls if you cripple me."

"So you're game?" asked Flower eagerly.

"All right," said Wren. "We'll go with you. But first we need some water." She tried to think back on how long it'd been since she'd had a drink. Back on Edgeland, before they got into the rowboat, Crown had offered her a sip from his flask. She guessed that had been, well, almost a full day ago. Maybe more. Her throat was parched. "Can you get us a little bit?"

"Not really," said Flower, shaking her head. "There's no food or water down here. Truth is, dehydration is what kills most breathers. Three days without water can do it. But the hunger is what drives breathers crazy. There were these three sailors I tried to help. Musta been fifty years ago. They were holed up in a cave on the Sun side of the island—starving. I was trying to find them a boat and some rope. Then one day I went down there and saw that they'd started a fire . . ." Flower pursed her lips and shook her head. "Their cave smelled like burnt meat. And there were only two left. It was then that I realized how desperate breathers get. It almost made killing them seem like a kindness."

Wren felt her chest tighten.

Flower glanced back at them. "Sorry—bad story. I can't get you water, but I can find something to wet your throats a little," said Flower.

As they neared the top of the stairs, Alec's coughs subsided. Flower paused and turned around to face them. "Once we get outside, there's a beach not far away where you can find some seashells. The moisture from the fog collects inside of them. You can probably get a few tiny sips of water, if you try."

Wren suddenly felt very thirsty. She had once seen a House Aron priest ministering to a nobleman who'd been found dead in the sand dunes of the Desert Lands. *Thirst is the most painful way to die,* the priest had said. *We shall treat his body with great kindness.*

Flower pushed open a door at the top of the stairs and stepped into a narrow road. Just beyond lay a rocky shore and, past that, pancake-flat water that stretched out so far that it merged with the sky, forming a tapestry of gray.

If they'd been this close to the water in Edgeland, they'd smell the salt, hear the crashing waves and the squawking shorebirds. Here, the air was stagnant, and both the landscape and the sea were featureless, almost as though an invisible weight were pinning everything down.

"That way," said Flower, pointing down the path. A five-foot-high wall made of packed dirt separated the path from the beach and the water, as if to prevent it from flooding. The path followed the waterline, along the back of several bliss houses. "You'll find your shells down there, on the beach, but be quick about it. I'll wait here."

"Aren't you coming?" asked Wren.

"I have to collect a bag I stashed around the corner," Flower said. "But don't worry. You'll be fine, just stay away from the cages—and *hurry*."

"Cages?"

Flower shooed them away impatiently with a stroke of her hand.

Wren and Alec headed down the footpath in the direction that Flower had indicated. For a minute or two, they were quiet, taking in this strange gray world. The earthen wall, the exterior of the bliss houses, and even the water were essentially the same color. None of it seemed real.

Alec looked back over his shoulder to see if Flower was still there. She was—standing as still as a statue.

"Do you trust her?" he asked.

"I try not to trust anyone," said Wren.

"Not even me?" asked Alec.

"Of course I trust you," said Wren, quickening her pace. "Anyway, do I have a choice?"

Alec hurried to keep up. "Even if Flower gets us the boat . . . I don't know if I can climb all that way," said Alec. "I mean, you climb all the time in the descenders. You're like a spider. But I'm not sure—"

"Come on," said Wren, giving his hand a squeeze. "One thing at a time. Let's find those shells."

They continued down the path until it dead-ended at a small pebble beach. Wren set off in search of shells. Alec followed slowly. By the time he caught up, she was already at the water's edge, holding an old conch to her mouth. The shell itself was covered in barnacles and dried seaweed.

"How is it?" asked Alec. He eyed the shell warily. Wren was used to eating all kinds of critters that she caught in the descenders. She once claimed to have spit-roasted a rat. Alec, however, had a far more delicate stomach.

"It tastes fine . . . there's just not much of it," said Wren, putting the shell back on the beach. "Like Flower said, just enough to wet your throat."

Alec picked up a shell and poured a modest trickle of water into his mouth. It was drinkable.

Wren's eyes roamed the beach, in search of other shells. She then let out a muffled shout and clawed at the ground with both hands.

"What is it?" Alec asked, peering closer.

Wren opened her left hand. Inside was a gold case that sparkled with diamonds surrounding a three-inch-wide sapphire, and a pale pink gem that glittered as if lit by some internal light source. In her other hand, she held an exquisite turquoise necklace and a few sunstones. Together, these jewels would be enough to feed several families for the rest of their lives.

Alec's eyes went wide and he opened his palms for the jewels. "Where did you find those?"

"I can't believe it," Wren replied, setting them in his hands. "They were washed up on the beach like trash. I guess it makes sense . . . there's nothing to buy, and most everyone's in bliss." Her eyes scanned the turquoise necklace. "All those people trying to take their riches with them, and wasting their money on fancy funerals . . ."

Alec frowned and placed the jewels back in Wren's hands. "Keep them. If we get back, you can use them. And you'll know not to *waste your money* on funerals." He looked away, not willing to make eye contact with her.

Wren reached inside her robe and stashed the jewels within a small pocket sewed into the lining. At long last, she was rich. Not that it mattered.

"Look—I'm sorry," said Wren. "It's not funerals that are the problem—it's the selfishness that bugs me—thinking you can take wealth with you. I mean, imagine how many graylings these jewels could've helped."

Alec glanced down the beach and spotted one or two other glittering stones. "Who could've known that treasure wouldn't matter down here . . ."

"Or that it wouldn't matter if you stole a ring from a dead woman," added Wren. She locked eyes with Alec, holding his gaze until he looked away. "Too bad Sami Aron isn't here to see this. I'd like to hear what he'd have to say."

Wren looked off at the water. That's when she saw the cages that Flower had mentioned: several dozen rusting boxes, almost completely submerged. They looked almost like oversize lobster traps. She squinted, then realized that the boxes were sea coffins, the ones that bone houses, back on Edgeland, made for the Boat People from the Southern Atolls.

"Those are probably the cages Flower mentioned," said Wren, pointing out across the water. She ran her hand across her scalp, feeling the soft tufts of new hair coming in. It was nice. A reminder that she was still alive.

"Do you hear that?" asked Alec.

Wren lifted her head and listened. A muffled gurgling was coming from the water.

The water around the sea coffins began to ripple.

"We'd better go," said Alec.

Just as they turned back toward the path, they heard a splash behind them. Wren spun and looked at the sea coffins again. The water was swirling and frothing now.

Definitely time to go.

Wren and Alec had almost made it off the beach when they heard a clattering noise, like a wooden wheel turning over loose rocks. They scrambled over the dirt-packed wall that separated the path from the seashore. The noise grew louder, then died down, as if something had passed their hiding spot and was now on the beach.

They crept up to peer over the top. A few dozen graylings were heaving and pushing an old ox cart across the beach. They moved together in fits, struggling for traction. None of them spoke or even grunted. Resting on the cart was another rusting iron sea coffin. Several long fingers were pushing through an iron grate on its side.

Then they heard a voice from within the coffin itself.

"Please!" wheezed the voice. "Please!"

The fingers jabbed out of the grate, as if pointing at the very spot where Alec and Wren were hiding. Seconds later, one of the graylings turned her head toward them.

# CHAPTER 23

Wren and Alec dropped to the ground, ducking behind the earthen wall to hide. A minute passed. Then another. In the distance, they could still hear the man inside the coffin, pleading with the graylings. But his voice became fainter and fainter. Silence returned. Wren and Alec decided to risk another look, and inched slowly up the wall.

The graylings had loosened the ropes that bound the sea coffin to the cart. Like an army of ants moving a hunk of bread, they worked together to move their weighty cargo. They lifted the sea coffin from the cart and marched it into the water, heading toward the other rusting cages that lay off-shore. As they splashed into the sea, water reached the bottom of the box and began to rise up the sides.

Again, the voice from within the coffin called out. In the absence of any wind, it carried far. "I can explain! I can explain!"

The water around the sea coffin rose higher, and its occupant began to babble, then scream. The graylings waded deeper until the coffin was almost completely submerged. When they reached the area where the other coffins lay, they released the box.

Alec and Wren were so transfixed that they didn't notice Flower, who had crept up behind them. She touched Alec lightly on the arm. Startled, he whipped his head around. She put a finger to her lips.

*Let's go,* she mouthed, tilting her head back toward Bliss House Forty-Seven.

Neither of them needed any more convincing.

Flower hurried back down the path, hunched over at the waist, trying to remain hidden. Her pigtails swung about wildly. She was now wearing a small sealskin backpack—the kind of waterproof bag that sailors from the north favored—and it bounced on her back as she ran. Alec and Wren followed on her heels. They hustled past Bliss House Forty-Seven, then ducked down a narrow alley.

"Slow down," whispered Alec, when he had finally managed to catch her.

Flower stopped abruptly and turned toward them.

"What was going on back there?" asked Alec.

"They were vanishing someone," said Flower. "Someone who got on Ember and Shade's bad side."

"Vanishing?" asked Wren. She rubbed her shirtsleeve across her dampened forehead, wiping away the sweat. "You mean, *drowning*?"

"Nope," said Flower. "I mean vanishing." She wriggled her shoulders, readjusting the straps on her backpack. "You can't drown the dead, can you? So how do you punish 'em? I'll tell you. You put 'em in a box and shove the box into the sea. There's something about being in a cage like that—underwater—it's much worse than being in bliss. They say it's like a never-ending nightmare. You can hear 'em crying under the water."

Wren glanced back toward the seashore path and shuddered.

"What'd you mean when you said that guy might've gotten on Shade's bad side?" asked Alec.

"It's like this," replied Flower, shaking her head as if annoyed by the stupidity of his question. "We're all stuck on this island, right? Stuck in what seems to be an endless purgatory. Shade and Ember tell people they have to say their mantras and wait for heaven to open its gates—wait and wait and wait. And if you don't follow their rules, well . . ." She motioned back toward the beach. "*They'll find a nice, cramped iron box for you.*"

Flower crossed her arms defiantly. "Only *we* think there's a way out of here. But we gotta find it."

"Who's *we*?" asked Wren. "You mean you and this Sebastian guy?"

"Yes," said Flower. "He's our leader. There are a handful of us." Then she knelt down and rummaged through her pack, pushing a leather-bound prayer book aside, and pulled out three dirty gray cloaks.

"Put 'em on," said Flower. "They'll help us pass as graylings." She handed a robe to Alec and one to Wren.

"We gotta be careful," said Flower as she pulled a cloak over her summer dress. "If the graylings catch you and realize you're breathers, they'll slice you up on the spot." Flower

134

paused and stared at the scars on Wren's arms. "I'm guessin' you already know how that goes. And once you're dead, they'll put all three of us in sea coffins—just like the ones you saw back there."

Flower looked at Alec and Wren. Evidently, she saw the terror on their faces, because she added, "It should be fine— we don't have that far to go—and the only tricky part is crossing the Meadow."

Alec cleared his throat. "Lamack mentioned the Meadow. What is it?"

"It's the most important place on the whole island," Flower replied. "Every so often, all the graylings and Keepers— *everyone* who works for Shade and Ember—goes to the Meadow to get Drops of Life. Without the drops, you end up like the rest of those sacks of flesh sitting in their bliss houses and repeating the mantra."

Alec scratched the back of his neck. His grayling robe was so stiff and itchy that it made his skin crawl. Wren never complained about this. But then again, she never complained about much.

Seconds later, Flower was moving again. They walked in silence for several minutes, continuing down the narrow alleyway. At one point, they turned a corner and came upon an old man who was pacing in tight circles. He was muttering the words of the mantra to himself, but only the last word was audible, so it sounded like he was just saying: *fear . . . fear . . . fear . . . fear . . .*

Flower raised her arm as a warning. The man had a rope around his neck, with a bell on it that jingled softly. He scratched his head as he walked, as if trying to remember where he placed his spectacles. He seemed totally oblivious to their presence.

"It's all right," whispered Flower. "He's in bliss—but he walks. Some people are like this—so the graylings march 'em around in packs. This old-timer must be a stray."

Alec remembered the sound of bells and shuffling feet that he'd heard before they entered Lamack's bliss house. He took a step closer. The man was ancient-looking, with a hunched back and yellow skin webbed with blue veins. Suddenly, he pivoted and changed direction, moving toward Alec. Flower grabbed Alec's shoulder and tried to yank him backward, but it was too late. The old man came at Alec face-first and smashed into his forehead.

Alec cried out and grabbed his face, and the old man toppled over.

Wren let out a little shout and jumped backward.

Flower seized Alec by the arm and squeezed it hard.

"I didn't know he was going to t-turn," stammered Alec, shaking off Flower's grip. His face was flushed and his hands were trembling, but he wasn't injured.

"Damn," said Flower, banging the palm of her hand against her forehead.

The old man was still on the ground, lying on his back. He was blinking furiously and making a gagging noise.

Wren looked at Flower. "What's wrong with him?"

"He's waking up," said Flower. She looked at Alec accusingly. "This is bad. Now they'll know for sure that there's breathers on the island."

The old man sat up. His eyes—streaked with red capillaries—were wide-open now, and his teeth were chattering.

"It's all right," said Flower in a calm, reassuring tone. She squatted down so she was eye level with the man. "We're friends."

The old man stared at her in abject horror. He began shrieking at the top of his lungs.

# CHAPTER
# 24

"What should we do to help him?" asked Wren, struggling to make herself heard over the shouts of the old man. He sounded as if he were in mortal pain.

Flower shook her head. "Nothing. He'll stop in a while, but we gotta leave. *Quick!* Before anyone finds us." They followed as she dashed down the alley. Soon, they emerged onto a wide street that ran parallel to the water-filled moat and the great wall.

Right away, they could hear the sound of jingling bells.

They were so loud that they could no longer hear the distant shouts of the old man. There were several dozen people about fifty feet away, all with bells hung around their necks. They shuffled forward slowly, mindlessly, just like the old man had. A grayling with a pointy wooden stick led them, pulling on a piece of twine connected to a web of strings that bound the pack together. He nodded in a bored way at Flower, Wren, and Alec as they approached.

A half-dozen other graylings, all carrying sticks, surrounded

138

the pack. At one point, an old woman started to stray to the side, yanking on her twine. A grayling prodded her until she fell back into line.

Flower drew close to Alec and Wren. "Keep your heads tucked down, chins to your chests, and breathe through your noses. It'll be over if you wake another one."

The jingling grew louder as the pack approached. Flower steered a wide path around the mob. Alec and Wren didn't dare look up. A few of the dead were actually chanting, almost shouting, the words of the mantra—their cries barely audible over the chorus of bells.

Wren expected the graylings to say something—*Where you headed? Nice day to walk the dead, isn't it?*—but no one said a word.

Moments later, Alec, Flower, and Wren crossed a nearby bridge that spanned the moat. It led to a winding stone staircase that rose several hundred feet to the top of the wall that divided the island. Together, they began climbing upward. Up close, the wall was stunning, mainly for its bulk. It looked absolutely impregnable; there were no cracks at all in the gray stone facade.

At the very top, the wall curved out into a bulge, forming a giant teardrop. Alec remembered seeing this as they approached the island. Green vines dangled down from its top; it looked like there might be a roof garden up there. So *this* was the Meadow. They were close.

Wren glanced about uneasily. "Why do we have to cross here?" she asked. "Why not swim around the island—or take a canoe?"

"They patrol the water," muttered Flower. "Trust me. This is the best way. We'll slip right under their noses."

Flower's steps were now slow and labored, as if she were very tired. Alec and Wren mimicked her. Up ahead, the staircase became congested with graylings and a number of people in burlap robes, with shovels and pickaxes slung over their shoulders. These had to be the diggers and laborers that Lamack had mentioned.

No one spoke.

The only sound was an endless shuffle of footsteps.

When they finally reached the top of the wall, they saw a stone gate whose entranceway was draped in fluttering silver banners. Here, the air was as fragrant as a spring afternoon. And there was a breeze. A real breeze. From somewhere inside the gate, they heard squawking noises.

"Hold your breath when we pass through the gate," whispered Flower. "Or the gatekeepers may smell you. Do *not* breathe. Even a little. I lost a breather in here once."

The line of people shambled through the gate and into a tunnel. Alec, Wren, and Flower inched forward. Each person bowed at the entrance, then ducked through the fluttering banners. Inside, the light was dim, but Wren managed to catch a glimpse of the gatekeepers. They were tall, burly men. And their eyes were sewn shut.

The Blind.

No wonder Flower had warned them to hold their breath. It brought to mind the old saying—the Blind could smell pickles on your breath across a crowded room.

It was deafeningly loud in the tunnel. The members of the

Blind were calling to another—chirping, squawking, and cawing—just as they did in the above world. To Alec and Wren, it sounded as if they were making their way through a crowded aviary filled with alarmed birds. Wren bit her lip and suppressed a shudder. She could feel pressure building in her lungs, and her throat itched. A cough was building. *Not now,* she told herself. *Please—not now.*

One of the Blind, a tall, bald man with a neck as thick as a sturdy tree trunk, seemed to sense her discomfort. He turned toward her and cawed loudly: *tssk, tsssk, screeee.*

Wren kept walking.

*Tssk, tsssk, screeee.*

The noise bounced off the narrow walls of the tunnel, growing louder with every echo. Wren focused on the back of Flower's head as she stepped forward. The burning in her chest grew. Soon, the tunnel ended. They passed through more fluttering banners and emerged into a great, open space.

Wren gasped, sucking in a few rapid breaths.

Then she noticed the ground beneath her—it was bright green—the kind of color that comes only in the spring. It was soft, spongy, and most of all, *alive.* She began to sink to the ground, still dizzy from holding her breath for so long. Flower seemed to anticipate this. She grabbed Wren by the arm and pulled her up.

"Not yet," she whispered. "Just a few more minutes. You can do it." She looked up at Alec, who seemed to be wavering as well. "It's nearly over," she added. "Now we just have to get past Shade."

*Get past Shade?*

Alec and Wren looked around nervously, half expecting to see the Shadow leader standing right next to them.

But he wasn't there.

In fact, the scene before them was remarkably . . . peaceful.

A slight wind caressed their faces. In front of them lay the Meadow: a beautifully manicured lawn, worthy of a nobleman's estate. At its center was a small cluster of leafy trees. After the gray sky, gray water, and gray buildings, it was remarkable.

From this perspective, they could see the Meadow narrow at either end and form back into the wall. The wall then continued in either direction, twisting and turning its way across the island.

"Follow me," whispered Flower.

She led them toward a queue lined up along thc Meadow's perimeter.

Shade stood in front, facing the line, resplendent in a robe made of moss; it was as though he'd cut it from the Meadow and flung it across his shoulders.

Wren tugged lightly on Flower's cloak. "What do we do?"

"Eyes straight ahead," whispered Flower.

Shade stood in front of a two-tiered stone fountain that reminded Alec of a wedding cake he'd seen when he was very young. The upper tier was a chalice overflowing with water, which dripped steadily into a larger basin directly below. The fountain stood on a carved stone block.

Shade held a dipper in his hand, the sort used to ladle soup from a pot. The line moved quickly and, before long, it was Flower's turn to stand before Shade. The hood on her gray robe covered her head, and she stared at the ground. Flower seemed to be doing everything she could so Shade would *not* see her face.

She reached out her hands, cupping them together.

"Thank you, Father, for these Drops of Life," she murmured in the voice of a frightened child.

Shade looked ahead, staring at the others in line, barely noticing Flower. In a practiced motion, he tipped the dipper slightly so that a few drops of water fell into Flower's hands. Flower took her dampened hands and rubbed them across her forehead. For a moment, her whole body trembled. Then she turned away and began walking toward the trees in the middle of the Meadow.

Wren was next.

She looked up for an instant and, to her astonishment, saw someone she recognized.

Oscar—her old friend from the descenders.

His brother, Joseph, had been desperate to find him, and here he was, at Shade's elbow, staring back at her. The two brothers had the same square jaw and deep, sunken eyes, but Oscar was bigger, with powerful shoulders and a thick neck. And his eyes had a steely glint to them. Mira had been right to fear him. He was a warrior.

Oscar's eyes widened in recognition.

Shade was momentarily distracted, refilling his dipper from the basin.

Wren brought a finger to her lips.

Oscar looked away.

A moment later, Shade spun back around and, in a quick

143

businesslike fashion, sprinkled several drops into Wren's outstretched hands. For a moment, Shade looked directly into
Wren's eyes, with a deep, penetrating glare. Then he gestured
impatiently for her to move on.

# CHAPTER 25

Alec was next.

He glanced at Oscar, but had no idea who he was and paid him no mind. Alec stepped forward, bowed, and offered his cupped hands. Several drops of cold water hit his fingers. He rubbed them onto his forehead, stood up, and briefly made eye contact with Shade.

A fraction of a second later, Shade's face contorted, as if he'd just bit into a rotten piece of fruit.

Alec forced himself to keep his eyes on Shade. *He knows,* thought Alec. *He knows.*

But it wasn't Alec whom Shade was looking at.

Shade was focused on the next person in line—an elderly woman who'd fallen to her knees and was using a shovel to prop herself up and get back on her feet. The woman's fingers were twisted and gnarled, as if they had been broken and re-broken many times. Her fingernails were cracked and blackened. Finally, she gave up on standing and began half crawling, half dragging herself toward Shade.

Alec walked away from the fountain, but after several feet, he turned and watched the scene unfolding behind him. The old woman continued crawling toward the fountain, grunting with effort as she grasped at the mossy ground. Shade watched with avid interest, like a spectator, curious to see how much farther the old woman could go.

When she finally reached Shade, he sighed theatrically. "Aren't you a tired, broken old thing?" he said. His clear voice seemed to ride the breeze and envelop the Meadow.

"I can still be of service, dear Shade," croaked the old woman. "I'm as hard of a worker now as I was a hundred years ago. I've got experience, too. Why, you should see me move dirt." She cupped her hands together, trying to keep them steady, but they were trembling as if she was on the verge of hypothermia.

Shade tilted his head to the side, unconvinced. "My dear," he said. "You have done your part—more than your part. You have earned your time in bliss. Now go and chant your mantras with the others. Onward to heaven."

"Not yet," croaked the woman. "A few more drops and I'll manage . . . I'm just feeling poorly on account of the drops wearing off."

"The dead do not heal," replied Shade with a shake of his head. "It's time." His voice was quiet, but there was an undeniable hardness to it.

The woman clawed her way forward, moving closer to Shade. He stepped back quickly, as if recoiling from a vile insect.

"Shall I ask young Oscar here to help you?" he asked, his voice now thrumming with an edge of impatience. The woman

146

reached out a hand to receive the drops, but Shade used the tip of his boot to kick her hand away.

Oscar's eyes fixed on the old woman. She flinched.

"No . . . no . . . It's all right," she stammered. "But please . . . let me crawl back to the gate. I should like to feel the moss of the Meadow under my fingers one last time."

The woman began to turn around and reached for her shovel, which she had left lying on the ground. Shade arched an eyebrow, as if skeptical that she could actually crawl all that distance. He looked beyond her, at the long line of Shadow penitents who were watching him.

"Next!" said Shade. "Step lively, now."

Someone tapped Alec's shoulder. He turned around to find Wren boring into him with her eyes. *Keep walking,* she mouthed.

Flower had set off at a brisk pace toward the other side of the Meadow. Alec and Wren followed. The scene here was far more peaceful. Shadows who'd already received their drops were sitting on the moss, like picnickers on a Sunday afternoon.

There were also, oddly enough, a number of stone statues in this area. This was the only artwork that either Alec or Wren had seen on the entire island. The statues were renderings of people in motion—walking, running, jumping—and they were made of the same gray stone as the wall.

Flower guided Alec and Wren closer to the dense thicket of trees and bushes that sat in the middle of the Meadow. The branches here hung down like thick braids of hair and were covered by razor-sharp thorns and metallic silver leaves.

Flower steered them around the thicket until they were hidden from Shade and the other Shadows still waiting in line.

Flower stopped for a moment and trembled, just as she had after receiving the drops.

"You all right?" asked Alec.

"Yes . . . much better now," said Flower. She moved her shoulders back and forth as if testing them out. "My arm doesn't hurt anymore, I can feel my toes, and"—she paused to sniff—"I can even smell a bit. For a few minutes at least, I remember what it means to be alive."

"I guess that's good, right?" said Alec.

Flower snorted. "It doesn't get any better for a dead girl."

Wren, meanwhile, was paying them no mind. Instead, she kept glancing back in the direction of the fountain even though it was out of sight.

"What is it?" Flower asked.

"I know the grayling who's standing next to Shade," replied Wren. "His name is Oscar. We were in the descenders together—back in Edgeland."

"Hmm," said Flower. She shook her head roughly, as if trying to regain her senses. "The man who drowned—what'd you call him . . . Dorman—does *he* know your names?"

Wren sighed heavily. "Yeah, he might," said Wren. "When we were in the water, beneath the falls, I said my name. I was just trying to, you know, calm him down."

Flower considered this. "And then at the harbor, Dorman made a big stink about you two being breathers. Shade and Ember must've questioned him. So we've gotta assume that Shade and Ember also know your names."

"So?" said Wren.

"So," said Flower, putting a finger on Wren's chest. "Your old pal Oscar just spotted you and, turns out, he's Shade's guard dog. You gotta assume he knows they're looking for you. Question is—do you trust Oscar? He could help Shade connect the dots. Will he tell Shade that he just saw you—up here on the Meadow?"

She glanced down at the scar on her forearm. "He won't rat on me."

Flower lifted her eyebrows and glanced back in the direction of the fountain. "I hope you're right. If the graylings start running at us, we'll know Oscar raised the alarm."

"That old woman back there," said Alec. "What'll happen to her?"

"If she goes quietly, she'll get a chair, like everyone else," replied Flower. "If she causes trouble, well . . . you know where they'll put her."

"It's awful," said Wren.

"And there's no reason for it," said Flower. "The water in the fountain is fed by some kind of spring, and it's *never* gone dry." Her eyes were tiny orbs of black. "But it's easier to manage people when they're in bliss. It's like keeping them locked up."

Flower moved closer to the trees and then sat down, crossing her legs and staring ahead with a beatific expression on her face. "Sit with me," she said, patting the ground. "We need to pass the time like happy Shadows who just got their Drops of Life."

Alec and Wren joined Flower on the ground. They had their

backs to the trees, but still they could feel the cold breath of the small forest behind them.

"The Meadow is starting to clear out," said Flower. "Shade and Ember don't want their Keepers talking to one another, so Suns and Shadows take turns up here. In a few minutes, there'll be a changeover. When that happens, we'll hide in the trees."

"Why are there trees here?" Wren asked. "And grass? How come the Meadow is the only place that's *alive*?"

"It probably has to do with the Drops of Life," said Flower. "The Drops revive dead things, and they must come from the Meadow before coming *out* of the fountain."

Alec stole a glance back at the dense vegetation. It seemed as if you'd need an axe to hack inside. He turned back toward Flower, studying her face. It seemed almost baby-like with her tiny nose, round cheeks, and big eyes. She looked so . . . *fresh*. That was the best word for it. It was the opposite of how he felt. He supposed it had been as much as a day and a half since he'd had anything to eat. He felt tired, achy, light-headed . . . hungry. For a fraction of a second, he recalled Flower's story about the three sailors in the cave. He shuddered.

Moments later, they heard chirping and cawing.

"The Blind," whispered Wren.

Flower nodded. "They're about to sweep across the Meadow to make sure everyone's gone. It happens before the change-over. We need to move."

Flower sprung to her feet and was at the edge of the forest in the blink of an eye. Then she thrust her arm into a gap between two thorn bushes and pulled back a large branch, creating an opening big enough for them to crawl through. After they were inside, Flower released the branch and they were plunged into darkness.

"Where do we go?" whispered Alec.

"Wait for your eyes to adjust," Flower replied. "Then crawl toward the light."

Alec crawled forward until the branches fell away and he came upon a small clearing. Slender beams of light filtered down through the trees. Steam rose from the earth and mixed with the muted light, giving the clearing a ghostly glow.

Alec and Wren glanced around at the canopy of branches surrounding them. Meanwhile, Flower sat down and leaned against a tree trunk. "We'll stay here for a few hours," she said. "Then we can head back out and leave with the Suns." She extended her arms and stretched, groaning happily as she did, like a traveler after a long journey.

Alec sat down cross-legged next to her.

Wren, however, seemed fidgety as she paced around the strange thicket. Branches of all sizes formed a cocoon around them, making it look like a small hut—about the size of Irv's place. An image of Irv, cowering on the ground as his hut burned, suddenly flashed in Wren's mind. She blinked hard and shook her head to make it go away.

"How'd you find this spot?" asked Wren.

"Sebastian did," said Flower. She was massaging her bad arm, the one she had broken, which seemed to be bent permanently like the bow of a violin. "Strange place, isn't it? The steam makes the ground warm."

Wren lowered a hand to the ground. Alec did, too. The steam made it seem as if something were smoldering beneath the earth. Alec picked up a handful of soil—it was warm and sticky, like half-melted wax—and he quickly brushed it off his hands. He grimaced, wishing for something he'd always taken for granted: clean water and soap. *A hot bath would be lovely.* No chance of that. He was starting to feel like a grayling.

Alec sat up straighter and turned to Flower. "I'm curious," he said. "You died about five hundred years ago? That was around the same time that Ember died, right?"

Flower stared back at him, unblinking, her big brown eyes shining like two glass marbles. "Yeah," she said. "I died with Shade, Ember, and Sebastian—we were all killed in the great fire. Half of Edgeland burned up. I was just a whiff. When we got here, no one paid me any mind, except Sebastian. He kinda took me under his wing."

"Wait a minute," said Alec. He leaned forward. "Do you mean *Sebastian Half-Light*?"

Flower nodded.

"Half-Light," said Wren, still pacing back and forth. "There's a statue of him somewhere. Didn't his family rule Edgeland?"

"That's right," said Alec. "They were a family of shamans who refused to call themselves Suns or Shadows."

Wren turned to Flower. "So you all arrived here, in purgatory, together?"

"Yes," said Flower. "The island was basically empty back then. But each day more dead arrived. Shade, Ember, and Sebastian took charge. They ran the island together—the three of 'em."

"Wait," said Alec, brow furrowed. "You said the island was empty. What happened to everyone who died before you?"

"That's the question—isn't it?" asked Flower. She smiled for a moment and her eyes seemed to gleam. "Well, they must've moved on."

"To heaven?" asked Wren.

Flower shrugged. "How should I know? Do I look like a religious leader to you? Point is—the dead can *leave*. That's what Sebastian figured out."

"What, exactly, did he figure out?" asked Alec.

"Well," said Flower, "when we first got here, there were no bliss houses. Those were built later. Originally, there was just the wall and what you see on the Meadow: the fountain and the statues. And there used to be a golden key lying in the fountain—shaped like a serpent."

"Used to be?" said Wren.

"Yep," said Flower. "You see, one day Sebastian comes to me, looking frightened, and says he figured out what the key does. That it opens a door—a way out of here. *Shade and Ember are after me,* he says. He also tells me that he has the key. *I put it somewhere safe.* Then the graylings came. They took him . . . and vanished him in a sea coffin."

"I don't get it," said Wren. "If there's a door, why wouldn't Shade and Ember want to open it?"

"Maybe something about the door spooked them," suggested Alec.

"More than spooked 'em," said Flower. "The door scared the hell out of 'em. Ever since they vanished Sebastian, they keep moving his body around, from one sea coffin to another. And they keep guards around it, too. Shade and Ember want to make sure he never talks to anyone—ever again. Of course, that's part of the reason why they hunt breathers—they're the only ones who could wake him up."

Flower reached into her sealskin bag and opened an ancient, handwritten edition of the Common Book. The margins were filled with notes in a tiny scrawl.

She tilted the pages so Alec could see. "This belonged to Sebastian," she explained. "He gave it to me right before he was vanished, so I could keep it safe. I've read his notes a thousand times, hoping to find a clue about where he hid the serpent key. But . . ." She shrugged and handed it to Alec. "Here—you try."

Alec paged through the book for several minutes. The writing filled every available space and was largely illegible. On some pages, it looked like one long, never-ending sentence. Alec eventually gave up and handed it back to Flower.

He looked over at Wren. Her nervous energy had clearly burned off, because she had curled up on the ground and fallen asleep.

"That's a good idea," said Flower as they both looked at Wren. "You should sleep, too. I'll wake you when we need to leave."

"What about you?" said Alec.

"The dead don't sleep—all we need are the drops," said Flower. She put Sebastian's book back into her sealskin backpack and zipped it shut. "But breathers gotta sleep. Go on. This is probably your only chance."

Alec slid onto the ground, near Wren. She didn't move—she was snoring softly, almost purring. Alec closed his eyes, but for a while he just moved around restlessly. Eventually, the warmth from the ground relaxed him, and he slept.

Hours later, Alec woke to the sound of moaning. It was Wren. She was sitting up, but hunched over and clutching her head.

Alec sat up and touched her shoulder. "Wren . . . What's wrong?"

"Dizzy," she whispered. "I-I think it's from being thirsty."

"Does your heart feel jumpy?" Flower asked, who was crouched by her side. "Like it's skipping beats?"

Wren nodded.

"You're dehydrated," said Flower. "As soon as we find Sebastian, you need to take the canoe and leave."

Wren shook her head and gently pushed Flower's hand away. "I'll be fine," she said. "Really, it's passing." She took in a deep breath and let it out. "Besides, there's something else I want to do before we go."

Flower tilted her head toward Wren. "Something else?"

"Yeah," said Wren. She looked at Alec first, then at Flower. "I want to find my mother."

# CHAPTER 27

Flower shook her head. "Bad idea. You need to *leave*, not start lookin' for your dead mom."

Wren cleared her throat. "Why is it a bad idea, exactly?" There was a trace of anger in her voice.

Flower returned to her spot, against the tree trunk, and sat back down. "You're not the first breather to get this notion," said Flower. "I lost *two* breathers that way. A couple—a mom and dad—wanted to find their kid, and I swore I'd never do it again."

Alec pursed his lips and nodded slightly, as if he agreed with Flower but didn't want to be too obvious about it.

Wren's face reddened. "It's easy for you two to say no," she said. "She's not *your* mother."

"Wren, wait," said Alec. He stood up and placed a hand lightly on the crook of her arm. "What happens once your mother's awake? She can't come with us to the world of the living. Remember that Flower was stopped from climbing all the way up. And if we get caught, we could *all* end up in those sea coffins."

Wren shook off Alec's hand and walked to the edge of the clearing, where she stared into the thick brush. Finally, she turned back toward them. "My mother died and I never got to say good-bye." Her voice trembled a little. "And my dad came looking for me, then disappeared. I don't even know where to find him—just that he *might* be from Ankora, which must have over a million people." Her voice was trembling more now, and her cheeks were wet with tears. "Even if I make it there someday, I've got no idea how to find him."

She paused, as if daring them to contradict her. Alec and Flower just waited for her to continue.

"Right now, I'm nothing more than a filthy grayling," Wren continued. "But if I can talk to my mother . . . just for a few minutes, it could *change my life.* She'll know where I can find him . . ."

Wren wiped her face with the backs of her hands.

"Wren, I understand——" began Alec.

"No, you don't," snapped Wren. "You're not an orphan. You didn't spend three years in the descenders. You didn't get cut up because you were fighting for food. You were lying in your fluffy bed in House Aron reading books."

"I hated that you were down there," Alec hotly replied, his face flushed. "And I hated myself for . . ." He stopped himself.

"For what?" asked Wren. She looked at him expectantly, holding her breath. "Why'd you hate yourself?"

Alec shook his head.

"Go on," said Wren. "Finish what you were gonna say!"

"Fine," said Alec. He took a deep breath. There was no turning back now. "*I* told Sami Aron about the ring. I saw you going into the cellar when they were washing that lady's body." Alec buried his face in his hands. "Sami knew we were friends, so he came to my room and said that lying for a thief is the same as stealing the ring myself, and that he'd send me back to my parents if I didn't talk. I was *nine*. I was scared, Wren."

For a minute, there was absolute silence. Wren sat rigidly still. Finally, she reached out and peeled Alec's hands away from his face.

"I'm not stupid," said Wren. As they stood in the clearing, she turned to look in his eyes. "I knew exactly what happened. I always knew."

Alec's face turned white. "*You knew?* But . . . why didn't you say anything? How could you still be friends with me?"

"I was angry . . . for a long time," Wren admitted. "Still am, a little bit, I guess. I mean, you did rat on me, Alec." She shook her head. "But look, you also stuck by me. You're the only one who did. You brought me food . . . and coins. I mean, I would've died if it wasn't for you."

Alec sniffled and wiped his nose along the grimy sleeve of his robe.

"The worst part," said Alec, "was that I believed you'd really done something wrong. I believed that people actually *needed* all their things in the next world. And none of it's true."

For the first time in a long while, Flower spoke up.

"There's only one thing people need down here," she said. In that moment, her eyes looked impossibly old. They were not the eyes of a girl—they were the eyes of a woman who'd lived for centuries. "They need a way out. And what you and Wren are doing—helping to wake Sebastian—it could save all of the dead from these horrible bliss houses." She stood up and walked over to the crawlway that led back to the Meadow. "I'm gonna have a quick look," said Flower as she crept through the thorn bushes. "It's almost time."

Alec rubbed the palm of his hand against his forehead.

"You knew all along," he said. "I always figured that if you knew, you'd never speak to me again. It's why I never said anything."

"I'm the one who stole from the dead," she said with a shrug. Her tone was now light, skipping over the surface of the moment like a rounded pebble. "It was my choice. I was just so obsessed with going to Ankora." She smiled and wiped her face. "At this point, I'd settle for going back to the descenders."

Alec turned his head, glancing down the crawlway, but he didn't see Flower.

"Wren," he said, looking back at her. "If we die down here . . ."

"We won't," said Wren. She sighed. "One way or another, we're getting out of this rat hole."

Flower emerged into the clearing. "The Suns are leaving faster than I expected. We gotta go."

Wren nodded. She felt better after her rest and was eager to leave. "We're ready."

Flower pivoted back into the crawl space, followed by Wren. For a moment, Alec was left alone, his mind swimming with everything that had happened. He wanted to call out to Wren, grab her attention—and see her face one more time— just so he could assure himself that she wasn't secretly holding a grudge.

But she was already out of sight.

Alec entered and crawled quickly to catch up to them. He found Wren and Flower crouched at the hidden entrance. They waited in silence for another minute.

"Now," said Flower. She pushed open the branches so Alec and Wren could step through. They walked directly toward the stone gateway that led to the Sun side of the island.

Once again, they had to pass through a tunnel manned by the Blind—but they moved quickly and soon emerged onto a broad terrace with a panoramic view of the other half of the island.

Alec was relieved. These were his people—Suns—even if they were dead.

The only way down was a long, winding staircase, which was now congested with throngs of Keepers returning from the Meadow. Wren, Alec, and Flower waited on the terrace until it began to clear. Dressed in their grayling robes, no one paid them any mind.

Directly in front of them stood a man and a woman, both wearing threadbare burlap robes ribboned with gold thread. Their arms, necks, and hair were covered with a chalky gray dust. The woman held a rusting pickaxe in her calloused hands. The man carried a dented metal bucket in one hand and was stroking the stubble along his chin with the other.

"Quit it, already," said the woman. "Enough with yer scratchin'."

"Leave me be," said the man, still caressing the bristly hairs along his chin. "Bein' able to feel things don't last long. I want to enjoy it while I can."

"Enjoy it," said the woman. "That's a funny way of puttin' it."

"You're just jealous," said the man.

"Jealous of you scratchin' your beard?" said the woman.

The man guffawed. "That's right. You're jealous of me scratchin' my beard!"

"You're a fool," growled the woman. "Anyway, a lot of good that'll do you, diggin' in the darkness."

The man's only reply was the sound of his continued scratching.

The staircase began to clear, and those still at the top, including Flower, Alec, and Wren, started down.

Wren could think of little else besides her mother. She knew that if she pushed hard enough, Alec would help find her. And maybe she could persuade Flower. But was it wise? Without water or food, climbing the falls would be a gargantuan task. *She* was a very good climber. But what about Alec? She thought of his manicured hands, suited mainly for turning the pages of a book. Could he really make it?

At the bottom of the stairs, they entered a circular plaza, which served as the intersection of seven converging streets. The crowds dispersed. Flower led them down a street that wove between several warehouses, each one crowned with sharp-tipped pyramids. Every building had a numbered door—these, clearly, were the bliss houses for the Sun side of the island.

The streets were by no means crowded, like in Edgeland, but they seemed busier than the ones on the Shadow side. Keepers in tattered gold robes stood outside each bliss house. Several eyed them curiously, but quickly averted their gaze. Flower picked up her pace.

Wren shot Alec a questioning look.

Alec shrugged.

Then came an unexpected noise. It sounded like rain. *Wouldn't that be nice.* Wren imagined cold water splashing into her open mouth. But it didn't seem possible. There was no humidity in the air, and the sky was the same white-gray it had been since they'd arrived. Flower began glancing about, as if searching for an escape route, but there was nowhere to go but forward or backward. Flower cursed to herself and motioned them toward the outer wall of the closest bliss house.

The sound of rain grew louder.

And then the pack appeared.

Wren could see them approaching in the distance. It looked like the pack they'd seen earlier—a great crowd of the dead, deep in bliss, shuffling forward. Only this pack had at least five hundred people.

Wren glanced over at Alec. He was already doing the drill: head tucked, chin plastered to his chest, breathing through his nose.

"They run their packs bigger on this side," whispered Flower. "They seem to have more dead who won't sit still."

The pack's members were held together by a web of ropes made from dried seaweed. Rope bracelets with seashell rattles were tied around their ankles, hissing and clattering as they walked. This is what accounted for the sound of rain. A team of graylings, each carrying a wooden stick, whacked anyone who started to stray from the pack.

It wasn't until the pack was almost upon them that they realized there was no way around. Even if Flower, Wren, and

Alec stood with their backs pressed against the wall of the bliss house, they would still get trampled.

Flower grabbed Wren and Alec and pulled them back down the street, into a small nook in the outer wall of a bliss house. It was just a foot deep and three feet wide, but it was big enough for the three of them. When they stood with their shoulders pressed against the back of the nook, they were effectively out of the street and out of the way.

Seconds later, the pack arrived, seashells rattling. Faces came into view—lips moving, mouthing the sacred mantra. Bodies brushed past them. Flower's plan was working. Then an enormous man approached. He was about seven feet tall, and he was moaning and muttering as if trapped in the throes of a sleep terror. As he drew nearer, he began to jerk his arms about, pulling violently on his ropes. The ropes, already weak from constant tugging, broke.

Suddenly free, the big man became even more agitated, pushing and shoving those around him. The pack surged side-ways, filling every available space. The nook offered Alec and Wren little protection. Bodies pressed into them. They soon brushed faces with several of the dead. Alec and Wren could feel cold, leathery cheeks and hard, bony chins. One man's tongue was hanging out of his mouth, and when it touched Wren's face, it felt as coarse and dry as sandpaper. She and Alec held their breath for as long as they could, but it was no use.

Looking back, Wren couldn't recall how many faces she'd actually breathed upon. Maybe it was three or four. But it happened. A minute later—when the pack had finally passed—she could hear their screams. A man was yelling, "Untie me!" And a girl was calling for her mother.

Flower set off down the street, walking as briskly as she could without running.

"We don't have much time," she said. "Soon we're gonna have all the graylings on the island after us."

A minute or so later, Flower turned down a narrow alleyway that ran alongside a bliss house. They soon came upon a pile of rubble. Flower looked up at them. "Don't just stand there." Her voice was clipped and fast. "Help me move these rocks."

Alec and Wren removed stones from the pile, uncovering a burlap sack that contained a rusty sledgehammer.

Flower took the sledgehammer. They kept going, passing by another two bliss houses, until the alleyway emptied onto a pebbled beach hemmed in by cliffs on both sides. To the left, on top of one of the cliffs, sat a wooden crane with a boom, a winch, and a rope—the sort of device one might use to lower a crate off the deck of a ship.

The water here was choppy, with waves forming around what appeared to be a reef about twenty feet out. Wren remembered this from Edgeland: On one side of an island the waters could be totally calm, but the other might have white-caps. Apparently, it was the same here.

Flower glanced up and down the beach, as if looking for something that wasn't there.

"What's wrong?" asked Alec.

"There should be a guard," said Flower. "They always keep a guard by his coffin. A grayling. Only I don't see him. We were gonna have to"—she paused, as if searching for the right word—"deal with him."

Wren turned to Flower. "Where's Sebastian's sea coffin?"

Flower gestured out across the water. At first, it was unclear what she was pointing at, but then Wren saw the tops of sea coffins in the surf.

"How long has he been out there for?" asked Alec.

"In a sea coffin, well, about four hundred years," said Flower. "But as I said, they move him around. It took me a while to find this new spot, and then I had to find a breather. Everything had to line up."

"Trapped in a sea coffin for *four hundred years*?" said Alec.

Flower nodded. "We should get going," she said. "It won't be easy to get him out of that coffin . . ."

"*What* coffin?" asked a voice.

It came from behind them.

Alec, Wren, and Flower all turned around at once.

A tall, lanky grayling in a dirty robe was staring at them. He had a pug nose and a broad, flat forehead, like someone had smashed it with a cast-iron skillet. It was hard to know how long he'd been there.

"You misheard us," said Flower.

The boy took a step closer.

"No I didn't," said the boy.

He reached into his robe and pulled out two items: a pocket mirror and a knife.

"Put your mirror away," said Flower. "We're not breathers."

"Prove it," said the boy, holding up the mirror. "Put this up to your mouths and hold it there. I wanna see if it fogs up.

They got a search going on. Sorry. I ain't getting on Ember's bad side and goin' to a sea coffin on your account."

The boy took a step closer. "You," he said, nodding toward Wren. "Go first."

"No," said Wren, who was now standing rigidly still. "We already told you, we're not breathers."

"And what if I don't believe you?" asked the boy.

"That's your problem," said Wren, holding his gaze.

"What if I think it's fishy that you're over here talkin' about getting' someone out of a *sea* coffin?" asked the boy. "Then what?"

"Hold on . . . ," began Flower.

"How about I give you a little poke?" said the boy to Wren. He pocketed his mirror and raised his knife. "If you're dead, you won't even feel it."

The boy moved toward Wren. His face was calm, but his eyes burned with determination. In a dazzling flash of movement, Wren stepped forward, seized the grayling's outstretched arm with both of her hands, and kneed him in the groin.

The boy staggered backward, but managed to hold on to his knife. He recovered quickly. "Breather—I knew it," rasped the boy. He snarled, then lunged, slashing his knife at her.

Wren dodged to the left, moving with the dexterity of a dancer. Her hands were in the air, fingers extended. The boy made another stab with his knife, and once again, Wren evaded the jabs, twirling out of the way. Without taking her eyes off the boy, she calmly said, "Flower, give me the hammer."

Wren extended a hand behind her, toward Flower and Alec.

"Here," said Flower. She pressed the old sledgehammer into Wren's outstretched hand. This handoff presented a moment of vulnerability, which the grayling seized upon. He lunged at Wren once again, thrusting the blade at her stomach, but Wren was too fast for him. As he went for her, Wren took the hammer from Flower and swung it powerfully, hitting the grayling on the arm that held the knife. There was a sickening crunch, and the knife flew high into the air and landed some distance away, splashing into the surf.

The grayling clutched his broken arm, cursed, and then ran off down the beach.

Wren turned and looked at Alec and Flower. They were both staring at her, mouths gaping open.

"Looks like you've been in a knife fight before," said Flower finally.

Wren nodded, breathing rapidly. "You learn a thing or two in the descenders."

"Come on," said Flower. "That was the guard. He'll be back soon, with others." Flower pointed at the hammer. "That hammer is too heavy for me to swim with. So, Wren, you better keep it on you." Flower marched out into the water, pausing when the hem of her dress began to get wet. The water was rough, not ideal conditions for hacking open a cage and dragging a body back to shore.

"Don't leave anything on the beach," said Flower. "We're not coming back this way." She pointed off to the right. "There's a sea cave around the other side of those cliffs. The graylings haven't found it yet. We'll be heading there."

She glanced up and down the beach once more, making sure no one else was coming. Then she dove into the water and began to paddle into the crashing waves. Alec quickly joined her. The water was a little colder on this side of the island. Wren took several deep breaths. She followed the others, awkwardly holding the sledgehammer with one hand while swimming with the other. She peeked underwater.

The seafloor quickly dropped away into a trench, and the clear water afforded them a view of the sea coffins that lay below. Hundreds of rusting metal boxes, each fashioned with grated windows that revealed the faces of the entombed bodies within. The sight was so unsettling that Wren inadvertently swallowed a mouthful of water, then poked her head through the surface and gasped.

"Careful now," called Flower, who was swimming beside them. "We need you *alive*."

As they neared the reef, where the waves were crashing, the current grew stronger. It became difficult to maintain their forward momentum.

"I'll go first," said Flower. "It'll take me a minute to find his cage. When I do, I'll signal for you to dive. Then you'll need to hit the lock with the sledgehammer. Just use its weight—you can't swing it when you're underwater."

"Okay," said Wren.

Flower dove. Wren and Alec peered down, watching her kick serenely toward the boxes on the seafloor, scattered as haphazardly as a spilled deck of playing cards. Several minutes passed.

"Alec!" sputtered Wren.

"What?"

"Turn around."

Alec swiveled his head to get a proper look. Walking across the beach was the grayling who'd attacked them. And he had three companions with him.

# CHAPTER 29

"They're going to see us!" said Wren.

"Damn," said Alec. He glanced around and came to a quick decision. "Follow me."

Alec dove under the water and swam toward the rusting boxes that sat along the reef. Thankfully, they appeared empty. There was one propped up on a rock, its entire upper half sticking up through the surface. *That's the one. Just a little bit farther.* He kicked savagely until he made it to the box, then grabbed the metal grate and pulled himself round the back, so that no one on the beach could see him. He exploded through the surface. Two seconds later, Wren popped up alongside him.

"You okay?" gasped Alec.

Wren nodded and spit out a mouthful of water.

"Hold on tight!" said Alec.

A wave crashed over them, slamming their bodies against the cage.

Wren looked panicked.

"What happened?" Alec asked.

"I dropped the sledgehammer," she replied.

Another roller crested over the reef and slammed them into the cage. More waves came, and for several minutes, Alec and Wren struggled to hold their position in the surf.

"We have to get back to Flower," said Alec. "It's been more than five minutes. Try to stay below the surface so the graylings don't spot us."

"How do we open the lock?" asked Wren.

"We'll figure something out," said Alec. "Let's go."

Alec and Wren pushed off the metal box and kicked back toward the shore. They swam underwater, surfacing for air in quick bursts. The beach appeared empty—with no signs of any graylings—but it was hard for Wren and Alec to get a good look. They soon spotted Flower. She was fifteen feet below them, hovering above a coffin that was nestled not on the floor of the trench, but on a ledge.

Alec dove and churned toward Flower. She pointed energetically at an old warded lock on the side of the box.

Alec kept swimming.

*A rock. That's what I need.*

When he reached the ledge, he spotted one. It was smaller than he would have liked—roughly the size of a big potato—but he grabbed it, heaved with all his might, and smashed it into the side of the coffin. The lock shook, but held. Alec felt light-headed. He had to surface. He grabbed Flower by the arm, pointed back to the surface. Then he put out his hand, gesturing for her to stay put. Flower nodded.

Alec swam upward in a surge of desperation. He angled

himself toward the surf so when he emerged he would, at the very least, be partially camouflaged by the crashing waves.

As soon as he surfaced, he spotted Wren treading water nearby.

"I don't see the graylings anymore," said Wren. "I think they're gone."

Alec nodded.

"What happened down there?" asked Wren.

"I found a rock, but I couldn't bust the lock open," said Alec.

"Give it to me," said Wren. "I'll try."

Alec handed her the rock, then held his breath and sank underwater to watch.

Wren kicked her way toward the bottom. Air bubbles sputtered from her mouth. When she reached the sea coffin, she hit the warded lock with the rock until it gaped open, then dropped the rock and shot back to the surface. She and Alec treaded water for a minute, gathering their breath, then swam back down to help Flower.

When they reached her, Flower gestured toward the top of the box. Together, the three of them pushed and pulled on the lid until it sprang open. For a moment, flecks of rust and shreds of seaweed billowed out, clouding their view. But then a man emerged and began to float upward. His thick white hair undulated like jellyfish tendrils in the surf.

There was no doubt about it. This was *the* Sebastian—the last descendant of the great Half-Light dynasty.

# CHAPTER 30

Together, they pulled Sebastian Half-Light to the surface. To Alec, he looked as rigid and lifeless as the coffin in which he'd been entombed. Although his body was buoyant, they still struggled to get him over the reef. Then they swam for some time. Supporting Sebastian's shoulders, Flower guided them down the coast and toward a series of steep cliffs in the distance. The cliffs jutted in and out, forming inlets that were narrow but deep. Flower navigated them into one such inlet and toward a small hole that peeked out at the waterline. Up close, it was larger than they expected—about five feet across. They pulled themselves inside, entering a large, high-ceilinged cave. The air was damp and thick with mist, but the pebbly ground was dry.

They lifted Sebastian Half-Light's body and set him down near one of the back walls of the cave. Alec and Wren collapsed into a bank of sand, panting heavily, while Flower seemed totally unaffected by the physical demands of their ordeal. She sat next to Sebastian and began using her fingers to comb the seaweed and sand from his hair.

Once their breathing slowed, Alec and Wren sat up next to Flower. For a moment, the three of them simply watched Sebastian.

"Wake him up," said Flower. "I've got your canoe and supplies here in the cave, just like I promised."

Alec looked at Wren, who nodded. He knelt over Sebastian Half-Light, inhaled deeply, then blew a long, steady breath across the older man's face. At first nothing happened. Alec took in a deep breath, preparing to blow again, but Sebastian Half-Light's eyelids began to flutter. His nose twitched. His chin trembled.

Alec retreated, and they all waited together in silence.

It was hard for Alec to imagine that he was really face-to-face with another titan from Edgeland's past. Sebastian's ancestors had ruled Edgeland for centuries, keeping peace between the Suns and the Shadows. Of course, there were periods of fighting, and during one such time, it was Sebastian who had devised the Rule of Light. He was a legend.

Wren started to cough—a deep, hacking bark that echoed off the smooth walls of the cave.

"There should be some seashells over there," said Flower, gesturing to an alcove along the wall, several feet away. "They might have a tiny amount of fresh water."

Wren stood up and walked to a darkened nook where the pebbly ground was moist with dew. There were a few conch shells lying about. She picked up two shells—one for her and the other for Alec. She managed to get a few drops of water from her shell. She then walked back across the cave and handed the other one to Alec.

"Thanks," said Alec, putting the shell to his lips and draining a trickle of water into his mouth.

"Sorry I've got nothing to offer you," said Flower with a grimace. "I guess I'm not much of a host."

"There's nothing you can do," Alec replied. "We'll wait for Sebastian to wake up and then we'll leave."

As soon as he said this, he glanced over at Wren, trying to gauge her reaction to the idea of leaving without seeing her mother, but she had a faraway look on her face.

"It'd be good if you stuck around for a bit," said Flower. Her hands were clasped together, as if she were praying. "Sometimes, if they've been in bliss for a long time, like Sebastian, you gotta breathe on their face a second time a little while later."

Alec glanced around the cave. The ceiling and walls were too perfectly round to have formed this way naturally.

"Who made this place?" asked Alec.

"Yours truly," said Flower, with a flicker of a smile. "Not bad for a runt like me, huh? It was just a little cave at first, no more than a few feet wide. But I kept expanding it, especially after Sebastian was vanished. I wanted a place to use as a hideout—and a spot to stash breathers. So I kept digging."

"Did you bring the sailors here?" asked Wren.

Flower's smile vanished. "Yes," she said, running her fingers across the pebbly ground. "After that, I didn't come back for a long time."

Alec and Wren looked around the cave again, as if seeing it for the first time.

Flower stood up. "Come with me," she said. "I want to show you something."

They walked across the sandy floor of the cave to a spacious alcove illuminated by a dim patch of light, emanating from an old, rusty lantern. The light was so weak that they barely noticed it until they stood in its meager glow. Here was a long, sleek sea canoe, with a wide hull and high gunwales. Sitting next to it was a small barrel.

Alec looked at it hopefully. "Is that water?"

"Nope," said Flower, shaking her head. "Those are Drops of Life—an emergency supply for me and a few others in case we can't get to the Meadow. Stolen, of course. And, no, you can't drink it. It wouldn't do anything for you."

Wren looked inside the canoe. There were paddles, a dozen coils of rope, gloves, boots, a grappling hook, and a small axe.

"It's all here," said Flower. "Everything you need."

Alec looked at his hands, which were already covered with blisters from rowing in the waters off Edgeland. How would he climb up the Drain with his hands like this? A sudden wave of uneasiness passed over him. He turned to Wren. "I'll give it my best shot—on the climb."

"Don't even," said Wren softly. "I'm not gonna leave you— we'll climb it together—the whole way."

Flower grabbed an oar and turned it over in her hands. "The woman who escaped was named Pola," she said. "She was in worse shape than you two—and she made it."

"If this woman really made it, how come we never heard about her in Edgeland?" Alec asked.

"Would *you* talk if you were her?" asked Wren as she ran

her hands over the smooth gunwales of the canoe. "Imagine telling everyone about falling into purgatory, where people sit in bliss and graylings are in charge, and then you finally climb the Drain and escape. They'd send you to an asylum."

There was a sudden moan from across the cave.

Alec, Flower, and Wren all turned to have a look.

It was Sebastian Half-Light. He moaned again, then began to flop about like a fish on a dock. Seconds later, he sat up and screamed.

# CHAPTER 31

The cave magnified and echoed the scream, making it sound like several people crying out at once.

"You're all right," said Flower, placing a hand firmly on each of his shoulders. "You're fine. It's me, Flower. Everything's okay."

Sebastian screamed again, then went silent. He glanced around the cave, startled, like a person woken by a slamming door in the dead of night. He had a long nose and dark brown skin so smooth that he might've shaved seconds before dying. The muscles in his face relaxed, and his features became clearer. He eyed Alec and Wren, then settled his gaze on Flower.

"You found me," rasped Sebastian hoarsely.

"Told you I would," said Flower. She grinned broadly, so that her cheeks swelled, which made her face look almost pudgy with baby fat.

"How long?" asked Sebastian.

"Hard to say," said Flower. "Four hundred years—give or

take a few. Shade and Ember didn't want anyone to find you. They moved you from coffin to coffin and had graylings guard the areas. Then we had to find breathers who'd stay alive long enough to revive you. Everything had to line up."

Flower sat down next to Sebastian. Alec and Wren joined her.

"Four hundred years," said Sebastian. He shook his head slowly and then looked at Alec and Wren. "And these are the breathers?"

"Alec and Wren," said Flower. "They'll be leaving shortly."

Sebastian bowed his head. "May your escape be swift." He tilted his head—first to the left, and then to the right—draining water from his ears.

Alec inched forward. "Before we go, I have a question for Sebastian."

Sebastian sat up so he was resting on his elbows, and nodded for Alec to continue.

"Flower told us that you found some kind of door—and that's why you were vanished," said Alec. "So what happened?"

Sebastian grabbed a handful of his thick white hair and squeezed some of the water out. He squinted at Flower, as if trying to see her better. "There was no time to tell you," he said. "I'm sorry."

He rose to his feet slowly. "We found the door by chance," said Sebastian. "One of Ember's graylings—a girl named Nora—discovered a keyhole for the serpent key. She'd been playing around near the fountain in the Meadow."

"You're kidding!" said Flower, neck craned forward. "The keyhole was right by the fountain?"

Sebastian nodded. "It was *in* the fountain itself," he said. "Hidden in the lower basin."

Sebastian squatted down, picked up a small rock, and sketched a crude picture in the dry sand on the floor of the cave. He drew two circles, one within the other. The bigger circle, he explained, represented the lower basin. He then pointed to a spot near the edge of the lower basin. "There's a round button here," he said. "It's impossible to see—you have to search for it with your fingertips. Once you press it, a slot opens at the base of the fountain. It's also hard to find because it's right at ground level. Once you insert the key in the slot, the fountain slides, as if it's on rollers. There's a ramp underneath it. We'd been down here in purgatory for some time, and no one had figured it out. Nora did it on her own, and she'd just arrived." He smiled. "Only a bored, curious child could have found it."

Sebastian stood up and arched his back, making his vertebrae crack loudly.

"Nora came and got us—Ember, Shade, and me," he continued. "We told her to stay put. Then the three of us headed down the ramp. It kept going and going, until, finally, we came upon a room filled with statues—just like the ones on the Meadow. There were drawings, too—what would you call them?—*mosaics*—on the ceiling. One showed the statues with breath coming out of their mouths. And a second mosaic showed the wall, cracking and falling apart."

Alec glanced up at the cave's ceiling and tried to imagine what the mosaics might look like. Then he focused again on Sebastian. "So what'd you *do*?"

Sebastian raised a hand, gesturing for patience. "Well, we looked around a bit, and Ember leaned against one of the statues. Wouldn't you know, it slides! As a matter of fact, all the statues slide and rattle around the room, like they're on a carousel. After the statues slid, a foggy air started gushing out of their mouths, and then the walls began to crack."

Sebastian looked off into the gloomy darkness of the cave, lost in the memory.

"So the walls started *cracking*?" said Alec finally. "Then what?"

"It didn't seem like the room was going to cave in—at least, not yet—but we stopped pushing," said Sebastian. "Mostly, we were curious about the air coming from the statues' mouths—it was moist—like breath. And then we got this idea—to run a little test, I guess you could call it. We brought in an old lady from one of the bliss house basements on the Shadow side. Back then, we'd just started digging basements and subbasements."

"They go down a lot deeper now," Flower interjected. "Some go down for miles. And you have to stay in bliss. No one has a choice anymore. Anyone who objects gets vanished."

"It's worse than I feared," said Sebastian. He glanced down at his forearms and noticed several rust stains from the sea coffin. He began to rub his arms, trying to erase the marks. "I can't say I'm surprised. Shade and Ember were always terrified that the island would become too crowded."

"What happened to the old lady?" asked Alec impatiently.

"Yes, yes, yes," said Sebastian, rubbing his hands together. "Well, we pushed the statues again—made them rotate. More steam came from the statues' mouths. And the old lady . . . woke up. Started screaming. The cracks on the walls expanded, like there'd been an earthquake. It was unnerving, but it seemed obvious that this was *exactly* what we were supposed to do. Why else would this incredible room be there?

"But, as you might guess, Shade and Ember were horrified. They thought this room was a poisoned gift—a temptation. They believed if we woke everyone up and tore down the wall, it would create a never-ending war—a battle among the dead where neither side could win because no one could be killed. The only answer, they said, was to keep everyone in bliss—keep them repeating the mantras—keep the faith that the gates to heaven would one day appear and open."

"You didn't buy it?" asked Flower.

"No," said Sebastian. "Not one bit."

He stood very still. His waterlogged robes hung heavily on his bony frame, like old clothing on a scarecrow.

"We argued, but I couldn't change their minds," continued Sebastian. "So they vanished me . . . and they vanished poor Nora, too. They vanished anyone who knew about the room beneath the fountain. But before they got me, I took the key— and I hid it."

Sebastian went silent, and in the pause that followed, the only sound was waves crashing against the mouth of the sea cave. Sebastian hugged his arms to his chest for a moment, as if in the grips of a chill.

"What if Shade and Ember are right?" asked Alec finally.

"I mean, if the wall came down, and everyone came out of the basements—like ants—it could be . . ."

"Very bad," whispered Wren. She was thinking of the overturned urn when they first arrived on the island, and how quickly Suns and Shadows began to fight.

"No—that's what they want you to think!" said Sebastian, leaning forward, eyes gleaming. "I *created* the Rule of Light. I thought separating Suns and Shadows was the only way to peace." He sighed. "I was wrong. That mantra: Drown the Serpent of Fear. It's not just a saying, something to repeat forever." Sebastian shook his head feverishly. "No—the Serpent of Fear is the wall that divides the island. You see how it twists and turns? If we turn the statues and wake everyone, then we'll tear down the wall and drown the Serpent of Fear. I tried to convince Ember and Shade of this." He paused to catch his breath. "This has to be the way out of purgatory. Not saying mantras, not sitting in bliss—but coming together, Suns and Shadows, to drown the wall that divides us."

Sebastian's whole body seemed jittery, fueled by the depth of his conviction.

Flower stood up impatiently. "We don't have a lot of time," she said. "We were spotted by a grayling on our way to find you—and we woke up some others by accident. Ember and Shade may already know you've been freed. We need to move. So where's the key?"

Sebastian smiled. "Of course. Do you still have my book?"

Flower reached for her bag and pulled out his old, leather-bound Common Book.

Sebastian took the book from Flower. He brought it to his

face and kissed the cover. "When I died, a thoughtful bone-house worker put this in a sealskin bag, lashed it to my body, and sent me down the Drain with it."

Sebastian ran his fingers along the book's spine, then pressed down on a small nick near the bottom. The spine gaped open, revealing a secret compartment. Using his pinkie, Sebastian probed the compartment, and fished out a golden, serpent-shaped key.

Wren couldn't help herself. She reached out and touched the key with the tips of her fingers. The key was hefty and shaped like a cobra, with fangs and a hooded head.

"Sorry," said Wren, pulling back her hand. "It's beautiful. I've never seen anything like it."

"It's all right," said Sebastian, smiling. "I had the same reaction when I first saw it lying in the fountain. I suppose Nora did as well." He gave it to Flower, then turned to Alec and Wren. "Can I help you with your canoe? I fear it isn't wise for you to linger here any longer."

Flower put the key back in the book and tucked it under her arm. "Yes, we should go now," she said. "I promised to help them to the base of the falls."

Alec helped Wren to her feet. "What do you want to do?" he asked. "You know, about your mother?"

She glared at him but then her face softened. "I want to find her," she said. "But it . . . it seems crazy. We have the boat, the ropes, everything we need . . ." She paused. Part of her hoped that Flower or Alec would interrupt and say they'd help find her mother—that it was worth the risk. But neither one said anything. Wren looked at the ground. "Let's go to the Drain."

Together, they carried the canoe to the pebbly beach and slid it halfway into the water. Wren climbed into the front, and Alec sat in the middle. Flower walked around the canoe, inspecting it, checking that all the necessary provisions were inside.

"Thank you, and may fortune shine upon you," said Sebastian.

"Will you and Flower go straight to the Meadow afterward?" Alec asked.

"Yes," said Sebastian. "I've waited long enough."

"I hope it works," said Alec.

"I think it will," said Sebastian gravely, holding Alec's gaze. "And if it doesn't, perhaps you will finish the job. Because no matter what—you'll be back here one day."

Alec nodded.

Flower hopped into the stern so she could steer. Sebastian grabbed the gunwales nearest Flower and pushed the canoe forward. It scraped across the pebbles and gravel until it began to float.

Together, they began to paddle, and the boat glided through the inlet and out to sea. They dug their paddles deep into the water and pulled hard to overcome the current. Soon, however, the current released its grip and the canoe was moving forward steadily.

"How long did it take you?" asked Alec. "When you climbed the falls with Pola?"

Flower thought about this as she took several strokes with her paddle. "Seven or eight hours, maybe more. You stay on one cliff face most of the way, and there are ledges to rest on. But right now, I'm more worried about graylings spotting us in the water before we even get there."

Alec and Wren couldn't see more than a few hundred yards into the distance. There was no rain, but a hazy fog hugged the water.

"Flower, thanks for coming with us," said Wren.

"That was the deal," said Flower, eyes dead ahead on the water. "It's always something for something, right?"

Wren was about to respond, but then a flicker of movement in the fog ahead caught her attention. She saw several long, dark shapes emerge, then disappear.

"Wait," whispered Wren.

They stopped paddling and peered into the fog.

Whorls of gray vapor drifted past.

Seconds later, they saw the unmistakable outline of three canoes coming their way, with three small grayling paddlers inside them. The clouds of mist drifted quickly, however, and the canoes soon vanished.

"Damn," said Flower. "We need to turn around. Quickly now! Wren, give me five hard back strokes."

Wren did as she was told. Flower, meanwhile, took several front strokes, and the canoe came about. "Good! Now, both of you—give me twenty good strokes—Wren on port and Alec on starboard," said Flower. "Hurry, we need to get back."

They paddled vigorously and, before long, saw tall cliffs looming above them on both sides. Alec glanced at Flower.

She was cutting the water with her paddle, using it like a rudder. The paddle looked almost laughably large in her little arms.

"Do you think they saw us?" he asked.

"No," said Flower stonily. Her face was all business. "But it was close. I'm surprised they had a patrol in this area. It's far from the harbor and the wall. They might be looking for us. We ought to lie low in the sea cave for a bit."

Wren saw the opening to their sea cave up ahead. They'd come full circle. She sighed. It felt like fate was pulling her back to the island. They drifted for a minute.

Wren turned to Flower. "I need to ask you something," said Wren. "How long would it take to find my mother's bliss house?"

Flower sat there with the paddle across her knobby knees, expressionless. "Do you know the month and year of her death?"

"She died in June," said Wren. "Four years ago."

"Welllll," said Flower, drawing out the word, as if postponing where it might lead. "She wouldn't be far. But it's not about whether she's close or not, it's about whether you get caught, or what happens when you wake her up. Right?"

Wren shrugged. "I guess." Then she pursed her lips and continued paddling. They moved steadily back toward the sea cave. The mist had grown so thick that it was difficult to see the walls of the inlet. Flower proved a steady hand, however, and guided them expertly through the waters.

"But if we went quickly—and didn't linger—how long would it take?" asked Alec.

Wren was so surprised to hear him ask this question that she fumbled her grip on the paddle and nearly dropped it.

Flower shook her head. "You've been down here for how long now?"

Wren squinted her eyes closed and concentrated fiercely, trying to reconstruct their entire journey and estimate how long each leg had taken. "I'm guessing it's been a bit more than two days," she said finally. "But I can't be sure."

"Two days," said Flower. She took another few strokes. "Well, two days—without food or water—and a lot of exertion . . . I'd say, maybe you have another twelve hours before you're in real trouble. So, you *might* be able to pull it off. It'd be an hour round-trip to your mother's bliss house."

Alec shifted his weight in the canoe, as if absorbing the weight of this news, and the whole boat wobbled.

"If you were absolutely set on seeing your mom, we could do it quickly if we went by tunnel," said Flower. She drummed her fingers against the boat's hull. "It's your call."

"Alec," said Wren. "We don't *have* to do this. You don't owe me. Sami Aron kicked me out because I stole, not because of you. He would have done it even if you hadn't said anything."

"I know," said Alec. His voice was quiet. She turned her head, looking back at him. "But I've been thinking about it— about your mom. As long as I've known you, you've talked about her. When you were saddest, it was always because you missed her. If she's close, and we get there quickly . . ." He stared at her, but her gaze was so intense that he looked back down at the bottom of the canoe. "If we don't at least try, you and I will *both* regret it. That's what I think."

Moments later, the canoe arrived at the mouth of the sea cave. The hull ground against the pebbly shore. The three of them stepped out of the canoe and began pulling it forward. Summoned by the noise, Sebastian Half-Light emerged from the darkness of the cave.

"Why are you back?" asked Sebastian, as calm and unsurprised as if they'd returned a bit early from a leisurely paddle.

"The graylings were out in their canoes," replied Flower. "And Wren decided she wants to wake up her mother."

# CHAPTER 33

Sebastian stood there and crossed his arms. "I thought that might happen," he said softly to himself. He closed his eyes for a moment, as if meditating. "Well," he said finally. "We better get going—we should do this quickly."

Flower turned and stalked off into the darkness.

Sebastian watched her go. "She'll be all right," he said, following her with his eyes. "She's like that when things don't go according to plan."

"I planned for this!" called Flower from the back of the cave. "I planned for everything. Now come over here."

They followed Flower's voice, which led them to the spot by the old, rusty lantern, where the boat had once been. Flower stood beside a long wooden box. Inside was a shovel, a digger's robe, and a torch. There were also fire-starting tools: a slab of flint and steel.

"Put this on," she said to Sebastian, handing him the robe and the shovel. He put on the robe, grabbed the shovel, and tucked his book under his arm. "And did you take a few of the drops from the barrel? You won't stay awake without them, you know?"

"Already did it," said Sebastian.

"Good," said Flower. "Well, if we're gonna do this, let's go." She lit the torch and led them to the back of the sea cave—to the mouth of a narrow tunnel, whose walls were nicked and scraped with the marks of pickaxes. The tunnel led upward, gradually, at a slight angle.

"You made this tunnel?" Wren asked. She was right behind Flower.

"It didn't take long," Flower said. "Must've been a century ago."

Wren glanced at Flower's hands and noticed, for the first time, just how deeply calloused they were.

"Well," said Wren, "I guess when you're five hundred years old, it all kind of blends together."

"Now you're starting to talk like a dead girl," said Flower. As they made their way down the tunnel, Flower's torch began to flicker, and then a gust of wind extinguished it, plunging the tunnel into darkness.

"Steady now," said Flower. Wren groped for Alec with one hand. Sebastian's cold hand grasped her other.

A few minutes later, Flower managed to light her torch again. The passageway continued forward, but there was also a winding ramp—off to the right—that slanted up. Next to the ramp, a date was carved into the stone wall.

"We're getting closer," said Flower.

Soon, they came upon another ramp, also marked with a date. They exited the main tunnel, onto that ramp, and soon came upon a vaulted doorway.

"Careful," whispered Flower. "There might be a glade Keeper in here."

They entered a vast room filled with crisscrossing beams of light, which were reflected and multiplied by a network of mirrors. The walls were sculpted to resemble the tree trunks of a dense forest, and the ground underfoot had the texture of brittle grass. When Alec and Wren looked at it more closely, they saw that it was actually a carpet woven from seaweed and what looked like human hair.

The most striking aspect of the space, however, were the networks of ropes that hung from the ceiling, forming a vast web that hundreds of bodies dangled from. Some were situated comfortably, as if reclining in a hammock or sitting on a rope swing, while others were hanging upside down or sagging like damp towels on a clothesline.

"Is this supposed to be the Sunlit Glade?" Alec asked.

"That's right," whispered Flower.

Even after seeing the reality of the Shadows' bliss houses, Alec was still dumbfounded by what was in front of him. He'd often told clients about what their dead relatives could expect in the afterlife. And this . . . it was unthinkable.

Alec shivered

Just then, a barrel-chested man—who'd been sitting perfectly still on a looping, low-hanging vine—stood up so abruptly that they all jumped.

"Building something?" asked the man, eying Sebastian's burlap robe and shovel. The man's voice sounded creaky and weak, but his arms bulged with muscles.

"Yes," said Sebastian.

"Rather old to be a digger," croaked the man. Apparently, he was the glade Keeper.

"I'm good with a hammer," said Sebastian. "Maybe you want to come down to the depths and see?"

"Perhaps, but tell me something first," said the man. He pointed a finger at Alec. "Why was the boy shivering?"

"What does it matter to you?" asked Flower.

"It looked like a shiver," said the man.

"The dead don't shiver," said Flower.

"I know," said the man. "That's why I asked. The boy— does he speak?"

"I speak," said Alec. He tried to keep the tremor out of his voice. He paused. "We've come from the Meadow. The drops make me itch."

The man took a step closer to Alec.

"Give me your hand," said the man.

"Why?" asked Alec.

"I want to feel your pulse," said the man.

"He has no pulse," Flower scoffed. "He's dead."

"I'll be the judge of that," said the man, still staring at Alec. "I just heard there are breathers on this island. Now give me your wrist, boy."

The man lurched forward, reaching for Alec, but Flower stepped between them. The man batted her away easily, then seized Alec by the wrists. Alec wriggled desperately, trying to free himself, until the man finally punched him in the stomach. Alec crumpled to the ground and let out a deep, guttural gasp.

"Breather!" hissed the man. He leapt onto Alec, pinning his chest to the ground with a knee.

"I won't let you taint this glade!" he cried, wrapping his hands around Alec's throat and squeezing.

There was a blur of motion, and suddenly, the glade Keeper lay sprawled on the ground. Sebastian had hit him with the shovel, the edge of which he was now pressing to the man's throat.

Wren knelt next to Alec, who was now coughing loudly.

"Quickly, Flower," said Sebastian. "Get some vines to tie him with."

"Got it," said Flower. In no time, she had found several lengths of spare vines, which she used to bind the man's hands and feet. Sebastian tore a piece of cloth from his robe and stuffed it in the man's mouth.

"Lie still," Sebastian told the man. "We'll be back soon, and we'll find you a nice sea coffin if you cause any trouble. It'll be a small one, so there won't be room to squirm."

The man went still.

"Come on," said Flower. She led them out of the room in a hurry. They entered another glade, brighter because of several more torches hanging from the wall. Here the bodies of dead children were draped across a web of tangled ropes that hung from the ceiling. Their small faces gleamed in the torchlight.

"Who are they?" whispered Wren.

"Orphans," whispered Flower. "They were on a boat to Edgeland, but there was a fire. I remember seeing them pass through the harbor. Ember said they were too little to be graylings, so she sent them here."

Flower continued across the room, until they came upon a stairwell. The wall here was emblazoned with a lone word: MARCH. "If your mother died in June, she'll be three levels up." They took the stairs, passing sturdy wooden doors at each landing. The first one was engraved with APRIL. The next was MAY. Then they came to JUNE. Flower leaned against it, and the big slab swung open. She looked at Wren. All was quiet.

"This is it," said Flower. "Are you ready to see your mother?"

## CHAPTER 34

Wren felt shaky. She pictured her mother's face and imagined introducing herself, explaining what she had become: a runaway, a thief, and a suspected murderer. *Done well for myself, haven't I?* And what, exactly, was she expecting her mother to say? For a moment, she considered calling the whole thing off.

"Be careful," said Flower. "And be *quick.*"

"Flower and I will stay here and keep watch," said Sebastian. "If anything's amiss, we'll call out. And if we tell you we have to leave . . ."

"Yeah, I know," said Wren.

"Are you ready?" asked Alec. He seemed to sense her hesitation.

Wren nodded.

They walked into the glade and took in the scope of the room. There were at least a thousand people in the nets, all of them silently mouthing the mantra.

Wren took a step back. "This is too many people," she said. "We'll never find her."

"Let's start at the back and move forward," said Alec. "The light is pretty good. We should be able to see the people near the ceiling without having to climb." They walked to the back of the room and began in the left corner.

For several minutes, Wren moved from one vine to the next. She wanted to hurry forward and cover the entire room quickly, but forced herself to be methodical.

At the end of one row, Wren stopped abruptly, as if suddenly aware she was being watched. There, perched on the vines, was her mother.

"I found her," Wren whispered.

She pointed to a brunette woman hanging from a vine, about seven feet off the ground.

Immediately, Alec was at her side.

Wren spent a long moment just looking at her mother's lean, angular face. She had high cheekbones and a pointy chin. Her skin was brown, like Wren's, and her full lips were almost purplish in color. She was mouthing the words of the mantra, revealing a set of gleaming white teeth. She looked surprisingly well, as if she were resting comfortably on a Sunday morning. Seeing her like this brought back a trove of memories. Images flickered in Wren's mind: picking wildflowers with her mother in the tall grass and foraging for mushrooms in the woods after a hard rain.

Wren felt a surge of pressure in her chest.

She began to climb.

She was aware of Alec climbing next to her, but somehow none of it seemed real. When they reached her mother's body, they untangled her carefully and lowered her to the floor. Her hair had been gathered in a bun, but wisps had come loose, and dangled around her face like the threads of a spiderweb.

Wren sat next to her mother, leaned forward, and breathed across her face. *Please recognize me.*

It didn't take long for her to revive.

Her mother's fingers began to tremble, then her eyelids fluttered and opened. At first only the whites of her eyes appeared, but then her pupils emerged and fixed on Wren.

"Mother—it's me," Wren whispered. "*Wren.* Your daughter."

Her mother's lips pursed into a tight seam, then her mouth opened. An arm rose, tentatively, as if searching for air. It settled on Wren's arm and grabbed it. A cry started in the bottom of her throat, then grew louder until it echoed off the walls. Wren expected this, but it was still horrible to hear. Soon, though, her screams died away and she struggled to a sitting position.

She turned to Wren, who offered a small, guarded smile.

"It's me," she said. "Wren." Tears filled her eyes. "I'm older now."

"Can it be you, Wrennie?" rasped her mother. "Can it really be?"

Wren nodded. Tears spilled down her cheeks.

Her mother gripped her arm tighter. "You *have* grown," she rasped. "How many years has it been since I died?"

"Four," said Wren.

"Four years," said her mother. She looked around, taking in the strange images of the glade. "My sweet Wrennie." Her chin trembled and she reached out to touch Wren's arm. "You're so warm . . ." A curious look came across her mother's face. "Oh my goodness . . . Why, you're breathing."

"I'm a breather," said Wren. "That's why I was able to wake you from . . . bliss."

Her mother looked around and saw Alec for the first time.

"That's Alec," explained Wren. "He came here with me. He's alive, too."

Wren's mother nodded vaguely at Alec. "I'm Alinka."

"Hello," said Alec.

"What are you doing here?" asked Alinka. She rubbed her eyes vigorously, as if making sure they still worked. "How can you be here . . . if you're alive?"

In a rush, Wren explained how they had fallen down the Drain, met Flower, and ended up here. "And there's something else I have to tell you," said Wren. Her heart was racing and her mouth was sputtering out words like a broken faucet.

"Father's alive," said Wren. "Or at least, I think he is. His whaling ship didn't sink or vanish or whatever. He came look-ing for me, in Edgeland, but we missed each other. I'm nearly certain it was him. They said the man had a large birthmark on his right cheek."

Alinka appeared shaken. Her hands were clenched into fists, and her fingernails dug into the flesh of her palms. "My goodness," she said. "I think I'd have a heart attack, if I weren't already dead."

Just then, Sebastian's voice rang out from across the room, calling their names.

Wren turned to Alec. "Go see what he wants," she said. "Tell him I need another minute."

Alec nodded and dashed off.

Wren took a deep breath. *Another minute? How about another day or another month?* She turned back to her mother. "I'm sorry, but I don't know how much longer we have. Alec and I are gonna try and make it back up the Drain. Tell me about our family. Is there anybody else? I want to find Dad. Would he be in Ankora? I mean, it's such a big city. Where would I even look?"

"Ankora," her mother said, nodding slowly. "Yes. We were both born there. My parents were spice traders. Your father worked for us—tending the gardens. The problem was . . ." She looked off into the dim expanse of the glade. "Your father was a Shadow, and I was a Sun  so we had to leave. The two families wouldn't accept it."

Wren sat back on her heels, struggling to process all of this.

"I wanted to tell you all this at the perfect moment," she said with a shake of her head. "You see, we ran away together and moved to Vilna, which is where you were born. We told the people there that we were married and never spoke of our families. Your father pretended to be a Sun. We farmed and fished. We were poor. I didn't care, but your father felt guilty. That's why he took a spot . . . on the whaling ship."

Wren leaned forward, taking in every word, all too aware that any moment might be the last she'd have with her mother.

"Listen to me," said Alinka. She grabbed Wren's robe, pulling her closer. "Your father had six brothers. They lived on the edge of the Songbird District—in Ankora. That's where you want to go. If anyone can help you find him, they can."

Wren glanced about, looking for Alec, but he was nowhere to be seen. She turned back to her mother. Alinka was staring at Wren's arms. At her scars.

"You've had a hard life," said Alinka very quietly.

Wren nodded.

"I remember when my ferry capsized," said Alinka. "At first, I thought I might be able to swim to shore, but the current . . . It was too strong. I remember thinking: What'll happen to Wrennie? Who will take care of her? They say you'll find peace when you die, but it wasn't true. I ended up here"—she gestured around the glade—"and went into bliss. But even then, I dreamed about you. Even then . . ."

Tears rolled down Alinka's cheeks.

Wren pulled her close and hugged her. Alinka's body felt thin, frail, and cold. And then Alec's worried voice rang out. Wren could hear him running toward them.

"WREN! I can't find Sebastian and Flower. *Wren*. Something is wrong. *They're gone*."

# CHAPTER 36

"Gone!" said Wren. "What do you mean, gone?"

"I ran up and down the stairs and there's no trace of them," said Alec, still panting to catch his breath. He glanced backward quickly, one last time, as if hoping to prove himself wrong. "I'm telling you, they're *gone*."

He stepped closer to Wren and her mother and held up Sebastian's book. "I found this near the doorway."

"Is the key inside?" asked Wren.

Alec opened the book and poked at its spine. "Yes," he said, holding up the serpent key.

"And did you close the door to the glade?" asked Wren.

"Yes," said Alec. "I couldn't lock it, but the hinges creak. We'll hear if it opens."

Neither of them spoke for a moment, reassuring themselves that the door was not currently creaking.

"Sebastian and Flower must've been caught," said Wren finally. "It's the only explanation. We were set up."

"You're saying it was a trap?" asked Alec.

"Yeah," said Wren, grimacing. "It's like Flower said, we gotta assume that Ember and Shade know our names. And they know when my mother died. I told that man at the harbor. They must've put the pieces together."

"But if it's a trap, where are the graylings?" asked Alec. "Why didn't they come for us?"

Wren's face was grim. "I don't know," she said.

Alec had a fierce desire to run back to the canoe. It was still there, waiting for them. It wouldn't take long to retrace their steps and leave. And how hard could it be to find the Drain? He glanced down at his hands. He was holding the serpent key, which Sebastian had left for them.

"Who do we give this to?" he asked, holding up the key.

"What's that?" asked Alinka.

In a few sentences, Wren quickly explained what Sebastian had intended to do with the key. When she was done talking, Alinka extended her hand. "Let me have it," she said. "I can try to find the door on my own."

"Do you even know where the Meadow is?" asked Alec.

Alinka shook her head.

"Then you're bound to be caught," said Alec. "You'll just end up in a sea coffin. It'd be pointless."

"He's right," said Wren, touching her mother's shoulder. A plume of dust billowed from Alinka's robe. Apparently, she'd been accumulating grime and lint for four years, like a forgotten piece of furniture.

"The way I see it, we have two options," said Wren. "The first is that my mother goes back into bliss. Flower says that'll just happen unless she takes drops. Meanwhile, we run for the canoe, paddle back to the Drain, and try our best to climb. It would've been better with Flower to help, but we've still got a chance."

"What's the other option?" asked Alinka, eyes brimming with worry.

Wren looked at Alec and Alinka, holding their gaze for a moment before speaking.

"The other option is that we take the key, run to the Meadow, and do what Sebastian and Flower were going to do," said Wren.

"No," said Alinka. The muscles along her jawline quivered. "Go to the canoe."

"And then what?" asked Wren hotly. "I'll tell you: The key goes back to Shade and Ember, and then it's more of the same. More bliss houses. More sea coffins. More mantras. Until one day, when we die, and we're right back here—in purgatory—dealing with these same problems—only we won't be able to fix things because we won't have the key."

Alec balled his hands into fists and rubbed his eyes roughly. "Wren," he said slowly. "If we go back to the Meadow, we'll probably die. You get that, right?"

"No," she said. "Not if we bring support."

"Support?" said Alec.

"Yeah," said Wren. "Like other dead people—who we wake up. Remember, we're the only two who can do it." She turned to her mother. "Is there anybody in this room who might help us?"

"Maybe," she said. Alinka looked around, surveying the glade. She then pointed to a nearby tangle of vines, occupied by a dozen or so brawny men in matching red tunics. "Those men are soldiers from the Desert Lands. If I remember correctly, they weren't exactly happy about going into bliss."

"They'll do," said Wren. "What do you say we wake them up?"

Alec eyed the soldiers warily. "Hmm," he said. "Might make them angry."

"I hope it does," said Wren. "They've been left here to rot. Forever. They *should* be angry."

Alec sighed heavily.

"She's just like her father," said Alinka, with the thinnest of smiles. "The man had the determination of an ox."

Wren walked over to the vine where the soldiers were perched. She turned back toward Alec. "Come on," said Wren. "Even if they don't help us, it'll make it harder for the graylings to attack. The more people awake, the more confusion in the room."

"Fine," said Alec. He joined Wren beneath the vines where the soldiers lay. Together, they began climbing the vines and breathing on the face of each soldier. Then came the screams—a cacophony of bloodcurdling cries. By the time Alec and Wren had climbed back down to the floor, a dozen soldiers were in different stages of consciousness.

"What's happening?" demanded one of the soldiers. He had been hanging in a vine close to the floor, and was in the process of disentangling himself.

Alinka stepped toward him. "Do you remember me?"

The man paused for a few seconds. He had short-cropped hair and a nose that looked like it had been broken several times.

"We came in together," he replied. "At the harbor."

"My name is Alinka."

"I'm Simon," said the soldier with the busted nose. "Desert Landers—Twelfth Regiment. So, tell me . . . what's going on here?" Other woken soldiers climbed down and joined him.

Alinka pointed to Wren and to Alec. "That's my daughter, Wren, and her friend Alec. They're alive. That's how they were able to wake you. And they need your help."

The soldiers were paying close attention now. Wren stepped forward. All eyes were on her.

"Simon—you've been dead for four years," said Wren, looking Simon square in the eyes. "For four years you've been hanging on these vines. Not only that. You've been lied to—"

"Lied to," said Simon. "What you mean, *lied to*?"

"I'll tell you," said Wren. "You were told to wait and wait and wait for heaven to open its gates. You were told that you'd be in a state of bliss. But look around you. What do you see? Worst part is, there might just be a way out of here—a way out of purgatory—and no one bothered to tell you or any of these other folks about it. There's a door—up on the Meadow. And we have the key."

Alec then held up the golden serpent key for everyone to see.

The soldiers all started to talk at once, but Simon talked over them.

"So you got a key," said Simon, with a jerk of his head. "So what? How do we know it opens the door out of purgatory? Why should we believe your story?"

Wren swallowed hard. She was about to speak when an agonizingly long creak reverberated through the glade.

The door.

Someone opened it.

"The graylings are here," whispered Alec.

"Simon, they'll kill us," said Wren, pleading. "Then they'll take the key and send everyone back into bliss—you and your men."

Simon looked uncertain. He peered at the door and took a few steps in that direction. A whirring sound sliced through the air. Simon shuddered, then grabbed his left shoulder. The handle of a dagger was sticking out of it. Simon grimaced, pulled out the dagger, and wiped the blade along his pants. "Well, lads, it doesn't hurt when you're dead," said Simon. "That's somethin', I suppose."

One of his men, a giant, bearded fellow with a barrel chest, let out a throaty laugh. He had a bronze shield in his hand, which he had apparently managed to take with him down the Drain. He handed the shield to Simon. "Use this," said the man. "Pain or no pain, it's no fun being a pincushion."

Simon nodded and took the shield.

There was a sudden rustling—like the wind stirring leaves on a gusty autumn day—and then Wren caught a glimpse of several small figures darting through the surrounding clusters of vines.

"Diamond phalanx!" yelled Simon. The soldiers obeyed instantaneously. They fell into a diamond formation—surrounding Wren, Alec, and Alinka—with Simon standing at the head. Another knife whizzed past, but it missed its target and clattered off the wall of the glade. Simon raised his shield. "Double-time," he shouted. "Don't stop until we're out of this stinkin' tomb!" He paused for a split second. "One, two, *three*."

# CHAPTER 37

All that Alec could see were the bodies of the large, beefy men who surrounded him. They formed a wall of flesh, muscle, and bone, protecting him from a storm of daggers that rained down as they charged toward the door.

They entered the stairwell where they'd last seen Flower and Sebastian. Several gleaming shards of metal whizzed overhead. The graylings seemed to be in front of them, farther up the stairs. They were throwing their knives downward and then retreating. Some of the knives missed, while others hit their mark. The soldier next to Alec grunted, then pulled a dagger from his thigh. Alec winced, but the soldier didn't even flinch.

"Keep going, lads," called Simon.

The soldiers pressed forward, surging up several flights of stairs and out into the middle of a street, at which point they came to a sudden halt.

For a minute, none of the soldiers moved, leaving Alec, Wren, and Alinka trapped within their formation.

"All right," called Simon. "Looks like they turned tail and ran. Go on, we can break ranks."

The men stepped aside.

Wren and Alec looked around cautiously. They were on a broad street, flanked by bliss houses. There were no graylings in sight. In fact, the street was empty.

"If those little devils are around, they aren't showing themselves," said Simon. He turned to look at Alec and Wren. "But I'm sure they'll be back. And in bigger numbers. So where's this doorway you told us about?"

Alec and Wren were both gawking at a deep gash on Simon's shoulder. He followed their gaze, then shrugged dismissively.

Alec stepped out into the middle of street to get his bearings. He could see the Meadow in the distance—and the stairs that led to it. "There," said Alec, pointing. Briefly, he explained about the fountain and the secret room hidden below.

Simon nodded. "We run," he announced. "Hold formation, and move quickly. If anyone falls, we pick 'em up and keep running. Dead or not, we leave no one behind. Understood?"

The soldiers nodded and set off with a shout.

The pace they set was brutal, particularly for Alec and Wren, who were exhausted. Their mouths were sticky and dry. Their heads ached. And the muscles in their legs were cramping terribly.

After ten minutes, at Simon's punishing pace, they made it to the base of the staircase.

"What's up there exactly?" Simon asked, pointing at the Meadow.

Alec described the Meadow and the Blind who guarded its entranceways.

"Sounds like a death trap," said Simon. "Not that it matters—seeing as though we're already dead men."

"What happens when they chop off your head, Captain?" asked the big, bearded man who had given Simon his shield.

"Guess we'll have to find out, now won't we, lads?" said Simon.

This brought a cheer from the men.

"I'd just as soon keep my head," said Alinka, recoiling slightly.

"And you will," said Simon. "As long as we go fast. Now come on—up we go."

Simon started climbing the stairs. He was in the front, followed by two of his men. Then came Alec, Wren, and Alinka. The remainder of the soldiers brought up the rear.

Several minutes later, they made it to the terrace where Alec and Wren had caught their first glimpse of the Sun side of the island. Beyond that was the stone gateway and the tunnel that led to the Meadow.

"Stay here," Simon ordered. He left everyone at the top of the staircase and crept to the tunnel's entrance. He approached from the side and, ever so cautiously, leaned in to have a look.

Alec glanced back down the staircase and saw a swarm of graylings climbing up, heading toward them.

It was just as Simon had guessed: They had come back—in bigger numbers.

Simon returned.

"The graylings are back," said Alec.

Simon nodded coolly. "Right," he said. "Now here's the deal with the Blind. They're standing in the alcoves—just like Alec said they'd be. I reckon they don't know we're here yet."

"They won't let us stroll through," said Wren.

"You're probably right," said Simon with a dismissive shake of his head. "So here's what we'll do. Me and the boys are going to run in first. We'll muscle the Blind back against the walls. Hit 'em hard and quick. There aren't more than ten of 'em. We'll form a gauntlet. Then Alec, Wren, and Alinka—you can run right through. We'll try to find a way to defend the gateway so no one else gets through."

Alec and Wren were still panting, trying to catch their breath.

"How long will it take for you to find that secret room of yours?" asked Simon.

Wren glanced at Alec.

"No idea," said Alec.

"You'll have to move fast," said Simon. "We won't be able to hold the Meadow for long."

# CHAPTER 38

Wren turned toward the stone gateway. From this angle, she couldn't see the Meadow, but she knew it was a stone's throw away—provided they made it through the gauntlet.

Her mother placed a hand on her arm. "You don't have to do this," she said. "Give me the key. Tell me where to find the stairwell. You could run. Maybe there's another way down from here."

Wren shook her head.

"I'm doing this," she said, eyes fixed on the tunnel ahead.

"It's time," Simon said suddenly in a brusque manner. "Ready?"

"Yes," said Wren.

"I'll run through with Wren," said Alinka. "But then I'll come back and help Simon. He's going to need it."

"As you like," said Simon. "Give us thirty seconds—then follow."

Simon and his men rushed into the gateway. The seconds

ticked by. Shouts came from the tunnel. Then a loud clattering, like falling stones.

"*Now,*" said Wren, as she exhaled and broke into a run. She, Alec, and Alinka rushed into the passageway, eyes ahead, searching for the light in the distance that would guide them into the Meadow. All around them, they could hear the dull thuds of bodies colliding. At one point, a hand reached out and grabbed Wren by the shoulder, but someone batted the hand away.

"Keep going!" yelled Simon.

Wren had just began to see the light of the Meadow in the distance when a huge man stepped in front of her, filling the passageway. Wren twirled to her left and spun past him. Alec wasn't as lucky.

The man grabbed Alec and held him high in the air. Alec got a quick glimpse at his face—ghostly pale skin, bald head, threads dangling from his partially sealed eyelids.

"Help!" cried Alec while kicking at the man's torso.

Alinka flung herself at the man's legs, as did Simon and two of his soldiers. Everyone crumpled to the ground. In the scrum, the man released Alec, who popped back up and scrambled onward through the tunnel. He ran as fast as he could, burning through his last reserves of energy, ducking and dodging as he went. At last, he staggered onto the Meadow, where Wren waited for him.

"My mom's still in there," said Wren, who was struggling to catch a glimpse of the battle that was raging inside the tunnel.

"What do you want to do?" gasped Alec. "We don't have much time."

Wren swallowed hard, then grabbed Alec's hand roughly, and pulled him onward—toward the fountain at the center of the meadow.

The great expanse of green moss was empty. The only human figures besides them were made of stone, but these statues seemed so lifelike that Alec and Wren couldn't help but feel that they were being watched. They passed a statue of a little girl hopping on one foot, a look of pure joy on her face. For a moment, Alec swore he saw the statue move.

*I'm delirious,* he thought.

Wren looked back, still hoping to catch a glimpse of her mother, but saw only the entranceway to the tunnel, with Sun banners hanging limply over it. A minute or so later, they reached the fountain. It was gurgling pleasantly. The water was a murky gray-blue—nearly opaque. Alec knelt down next to the lower basin and pushed the sleeve of his robe far up his left arm. He then dipped his arm into the basin and began groping around the bottom, searching for the round button that Sebastian had described.

"Did you find it?" Wren asked, looking back at the Sun entrance. No one was running toward them—a good sign— but she could hear muffled shouts coming from the gateway.

"Don't feel anything," Alec muttered.

He kept probing. The bottom of the basin was uniformly smooth. He explored it thoroughly, and then did it again. A full minute went by.

"Alec?"

"Not yet!" he replied.

Suddenly, his fingers grazed a slight bump in the fountain. He froze. *This has to be it*. He pressed down as hard as he could. A loud click echoed from below the fountain.

"That sounded promising," said Wren.

Alec sat back on his heels. "I guess so," he said. "Strange— it didn't feel like a button at all."

Wren circled the fountain quickly, looking for the slot with the keyhole. She recalled Sebastian's words: *It's very hard to see, because it's right at ground level*. It took Wren another minute or so to find the slot. It was tiny—just two inches long and half an inch wide. She quickly slid the serpent key inside and turned it.

"Ready?" she asked.

Together, Alec and Wren pushed on the fountain. It moved, just like Sebastian said it would. The fountain and pedestal slid sideways, as if on rollers, revealing a narrow ramp under- neath. Bluish mist billowed out.

Alec and Wren hesitated only for a moment.

"I'll go first," said Wren. She hurried down the ramp, with Alec right behind her. Within seconds, mist and darkness had enveloped them.

# CHAPTER 39

At first it was too dark to see anything, but soon their eyes adjusted. The ramp spiraled downward, along a smooth, corkscrew-like passageway. The sound of their footsteps echoed off the stone walls. The air was so moist that droplets of water ran along the walls and dripped from the ceiling, stinging their skin like icy pinpricks.

They arrived in a circular room. The ground was carpeted with mist, making it impossible to see the floor. A dozen people were already standing around the room's perimeter, hands pushing against the wall. One tense moment later, Alec and Wren realized these were statues, not actual people. Their mouths were all open, as if screaming or singing—just like the statues on the Meadow.

Wren dipped a foot into the mist. To her relief, she discovered that it was only a foot deep, and the floor beneath was solid.

Alec glanced back up the ramp, half expecting to see a grayling there. *They'll find us soon enough.* He walked over to the nearest of the statues. It was a likeness of a young boy

220

leaning forward, muscled and tense, heaving all of his weight against the wall. The boy wore a robe emblazoned with the words of various Shadow prayers. The statue next to the boy was of a young man in a Sun robe, but in the same pose.

On the ceiling, just as Sebastian had described, they saw an elaborate mosaic with two images. One showed the statues with currents of air blowing from their mouths; the other showed a crumbling wall.

"Sebastian said we had to push the nearby statues—make them move—any idea how we're going to do that?" asked Alec.

"Here," said Wren, gesturing to the statue of an old woman. This was the only statue in the room that wasn't facing the wall. Instead, she had her back to the wall, and was facing the center of the room. She was holding out her hands, as if offering some invisible gift.

Wren took hold of the old woman's cold stone hands. She pushed on them, as if she were trying to topple the statue onto its side. Nothing. She pressed harder. Suddenly, the statue of the old woman—and all the statues—slid clockwise by a foot. There was a hissing sound, and white steam trickled from their stone mouths.

"Wait," said Alec. He crouched down by the old woman's feet and felt two parallel grooves carved into the ground. He followed them with his fingers, crawling forward as he did. The grooves ran around the room's perimeter. It was as he suspected: The statues were attached to a stone track, allowing them to move like the horses on a hand-pushed carousel.

"Try again," he told Wren.

Wren heaved, and the statues slid forward another foot.

Hissing filled the room, and more steam seeped out from the statues' mouths. Alec noticed that several cracks had appeared near the bottom of the wall.

"Did you see the steam?" asked Wren excitedly. "It's like your breath on a cold day."

"The breath of life," whispered Alec.

Together they pushed on the statue of the old woman, even harder this time. All the statues moved several feet more. Their hands scraped loudly against the walls, causing hairline cracks to race their way up the stonework.

"This is it!" Wren exclaimed. She ran the palm of her hand against the wall, and then looked at Alec. "Should we . . . I mean . . . should we really do this? We're going to tear down the wall—and wake the whole island up. It's going to be . . ." She shuddered.

"I know," said Alec. His legs and arms hurt; his throat was painfully dry. "I'm scared too," he said. "But we gotta do it."

Wren's head jerked suddenly. She looked back at the ramp.

"What is it?" asked Alec.

"They're here," said Wren quietly.

"Huh?" said Alec. "How do you know?"

"I just do," whispered Wren. "It's like in the descenders . . . You just know."

As if on cue, the mist on the floor began to churn. It was as if something—a great many things, perhaps—were moving beneath the mist, like eels squirming beneath the murky waters of a swamp.

Something grazed Alec's leg. He looked down, and a small pale hand emerged from the mist.

# CHAPTER
# 40

A grayling rose from the floor. Clouds of vapor rolled off his shoulders and twirled around him. He was about eight—very skinny, with light brown skin stretched tightly around sinew and bone. He was so thin and gangly that he looked like a marionette without the strings. The boy glared at Alec with such intensity that Alec flinched.

Dozens more graylings emerged from the ramp, streaming into the room and forming a tight semicircle around Alec and Wren—their grubby gray robes blending together in a great tapestry of filth.

And then Shade's voice filled the space. "Hello there," he called. "Looks like we're just in time."

Shade was standing where the ramp entered the room. He was wearing his robe of silver ribbons, just as he had been when Alec and Wren had first seen him. Ember stood next to him, wrapped in a glittering gold shawl.

Shade glanced about the room, eying his graylings with satisfaction, like a proud kennel master.

"Graylings are such obedient and loyal creatures," observed Shade. "And you know the funny thing? It doesn't take much to earn their loyalty. They were so despised in the above world—yearning to be accepted. So we accepted them. I suppose you can appreciate that, Wren, can't you?"

If Wren was surprised to hear her name, she didn't show it. She merely pursed her lips.

"We keep careful track of things down here," said Shade. "I know your name. I know your mother's name, and how she died, and where she is right now. I also know why everyone in Edgeland wants to catch you."

"I didn't kill Fat Freddy," she replied in a measured voice.

"Oh, I know you didn't kill Friderik," said Shade. "I've spoken with him. The problem is that no one above—in the world of the living—knows it." He smiled, but only with his lips. His eyes were lifeless and indifferent. "Perhaps you should consider staying here instead?"

"Yes, think about it, Wren," added Ember. "We could use someone like you."

Shade and Ember glided across the room toward Wren and Alec, moving so fluidly that they seemed to be floating on the mist. The graylings made room for them in the tight semicircle of bodies that surrounded Alec and Wren.

With Shade at her side, Ember smiled fondly at Wren. Then she turned to Alec and addressed him as if they were old friends. "Alec," she said. "Dorman told me about you. He said you worked at House Aron. I suppose that means you know who I am."

Alec nodded. Despite everything he'd seen on this island

and how wretched he knew this place to be, he couldn't help but feel a flicker of hope that—somehow—there had been some horrible misunderstanding, and Ember was not really to blame.

"Do I look like the founder of House Aron?" she asked, letting out a warm, melodious laugh.

"You look exactly like your portrait," said Alec finally. He tried to squelch the tremor in his throat.

"You mean the one of me standing in the sunlight?" asked Ember. "Do they still have it in the chapel—beneath the stained-glass windows?"

Alec nodded.

"Oh, I'm glad," said Ember. She seemed genuinely pleased. "I never much liked that portrait. I looked too serious. Kind of fussy, wouldn't you say? But I liked that spot very much. The servants used to serve cardamom tea there during the sunrise. Do they still do that?"

"They do," said Alec, nodding. It seemed bizarre to be chatting with Ember at this moment, but he couldn't help himself. He wanted to talk to her.

"I know you have a lot of questions," said Ember. "Both of you," she added, glancing at Wren for the first time. "Much of what you've seen down here must seem strange—sinister even—so I'm glad that we finally have the chance to talk." She paused for a moment and adjusted the fine gold cloth of her shawl. "So, is there anything that you'd like to know?"

"Where's my mother?" demanded Wren, eyes narrowed.

"She's safe and sound," replied Ember. "As are the soldiers you woke up, and of course Flower and Sebastian. In fact, I'm looking forward to chatting with Flower. She proved quite good at eluding us over the years." Ember returned her gaze to Alec. "What about you, Alec, isn't there anything you want to know?"

Alec looked up at the mosaic on the ceiling.

"Well?" asked Ember patiently.

"Aren't you curious?" he asked, gesturing around at the statues. "About what this room could do?"

"You mean tear down the wall?" said Ember. "Revive the dead?" She laughed again, that same warm chuckle. "My dear boy, why would we possibly want to do that? I suppose Sebastian has put some silly notion in your head about this being the way out of here—the doorstep to heaven—or some such nonsense. Oh dear. This is precisely why we had to vanish him." She clucked her tongue in a scolding fashion, like an old schoolmarm. "Can you imagine the horror that this island would become? A great war—Suns versus Shadows— the dead tearing one another apart, limb by limb.

"Let me tell you *why* we built the bliss houses," continued Ember. "When we first arrived here, there were fewer of us, and we all took the drops. And do you know what happened? Everyone was wide-awake and filled with dread. *Why are we all together—Suns and Shadows? How long must we stay here? Where is God?* People tried to end their own lives again and again—only they couldn't—because they were already dead."

Her eyes were fixed on Alec, but then they flicked over to Wren, taking in her shocked expression.

"Yes," said Ember. "It's true. And the bodies just kept floating ashore . . . hundreds and thousands of them. It was chaos. And then we hit upon the solution. Prayer. Meditation. People began saying the mantra and drifting into bliss. Right away, you could see the island changing into something that was much, much better."

"I gotta tell you," said Wren. She glanced back toward the ramp. "It doesn't look that great to me out there."

"Well," said Ember, with her kindly smile. "We haven't made it to heaven yet, have we?"

"But do you really believe that muttering the mantra will get you there?" asked Alec.

"Of course," replied Ember, clasping her hands together. "That's the nature of faith. You must believe in order for it to work . . . Alec, you of all people should understand what we're doing here. Why, it's *exactly* the same thing that you have done your entire life at House Aron. When people arrived at our doorstep—stricken with grief and fear—we gave them comfort. Comfort and certainty in the face of the unknown."

"It's not the same!" said Alec.

His aggressive tone startled the graylings, who perked up and inched forward like a pack of hunting dogs.

"*Not now,*" said Shade.

A fraction of a second later, one of the graylings—a big stocky boy—raised his hand. Instantly, the other graylings stood down.

It was Oscar.

He was standing directly next to Shade, though he gave no indication—whatsoever—that he knew or even cared who Wren was.

Wren glanced about nervously, taking in the faces of the

other graylings who surrounded them. Wren knew just how vicious graylings could be. She'd seen them do terrible things to one another in the descenders, especially when food was scarce. But she also noticed that these graylings weren't taking their cues from Shade. Their eyes were trained on Oscar. He seemed to be the top dog. It all made sense. He was just like Mira—the girl who ran their old pack on Edgeland.

Wren stared at Oscar, hoping for a flicker of acknowledgment.

But he offered nothing—just a vacant gaze from two unblinking eyes.

# CHAPTER
# 41

Ember stepped closer to Alec and Wren, her long arms clasped in front of her. They were only a few feet apart.

She focused her attention on Alec. "My dear, sweet boy," she said. "We're from the same House. You understand what that means, right? We're family. We must help each other. And now you can help us make this a better place."

Wren watched her approach Alec. His eyes seemed glazed over. Maybe it was just the hunger and the thirst, but he seemed caught in a trance. He even swayed back and forth, as if dizzy. Wren was feeling it, too. She glanced back at Oscar, but he wore the same mask of indifference.

"What do you say, Alec?" asked Shade. His deep voice purred, but beneath it was a slight edge, as if he were slowly losing his patience. "Do you understand now just how dangerous this room is—how *evil*—and why we've worked so hard to keep it a secret?"

"Alec, there's a place for you here," said Ember. She turned to Wren for a second. "A place for both of you. Just think,

Wren, down here you won't have to worry about proving your innocence. You can just lounge in the Meadow . . . with your mother, for as long as you like. What could be better than that?"

Wren bit her lip.

Ember reached into her robe and pulled out a long dagger with a razor-thin blade, then extended her arm and offered it to them.

Alec and Wren each took a small step backward. They were now almost up against the statue of the old woman.

"This is the only choice, my dears," said Ember. "But it's easier if you do it yourself, isn't it?"

Ember and Alec stared at each other, as if they were the only two people on the island.

"What are you thinking, Alec?" asked Ember.

"Well," said Alec softly. "I think . . . Well, I think you've made a mess of things down here. Maybe, once, you had good intentions . . . but this can't be the answer. I see no good in what you've done."

Wren grabbed Alec's hand and squeezed it.

"We've seen your bliss houses," said Wren, voice trembling. "We've seen those people crying in their sleep. And we've seen the sea coffins where you keep people like Sebastian Half-Light."

Shade scowled at her.

"I've heard enough," said Shade. He turned to Oscar and nodded his head, ever so slightly.

"Oscar!" shouted Wren.

Shade blanched, evidently startled that Wren knew Oscar's name.

"They're using *all* of you!" cried Wren. "I am a grayling, too—spent all my nights in the descenders, just like you. I was afraid all the time. That's why Shade and Ember picked you." She swiveled her head, trying to make eye contact with as many of the graylings as she could. Some refused to look at her, but others leaned in closer. She turned to Shade. "As you said, we're easy pickings—aren't we?"

"Shut your mouth!" barked Shade, flicking his cloak behind him.

"There was a grayling—a girl named Nora—she's the one who found this room," shouted Wren, ignoring him. "Maybe you remember her? They vanished Nora to make sure she wouldn't talk! They're afraid of this room. Because it leads somewhere else—to a place where they're not in charge!"

Oscar stepped away from Shade. He held up his hand, gesturing for the graylings to wait. Alec and Wren both tensed. The instinct to run was overwhelming, but there was no escape.

"It's time, Oscar," said Shade. "You know what to do."

"Yes," said Oscar, nodding.

The graylings reached into their robes and pulled out knives so small that it would take countless stabs to kill a person.

A painful death.

"I'll see you on the other side," said Ember, with a tremor in her voice. "Good-bye." She retreated backward, removing herself from the tight semicircle of graylings.

"Go on," said Shade. He was looking directly at Oscar. "When you're done, take their bodies back to the Drain."

The other graylings eyed Oscar.

He took a step forward. The graylings followed his lead, edging closer.

Wren squeezed Alec's hand tighter. "OSCAR!" she yelled. "PLEASE!"

Oscar brandished his knife and took one more step. He glanced to his left and his right, taking in the graylings behind him.

"Grab the boy," shouted Oscar, pointing his finger at Alec. "But don't cut him."

Several graylings surged forward, jumping on Alec and bringing him to the ground. Alec was shouting and struggling, until a grayling clamped her hand across his mouth, and another one grabbed his throat.

Oscar walked behind Wren and threw an arm around her chest, pinning her close to him. The other hand—the one holding the dagger—rose toward her throat.

"Oscar . . . please . . . we just have to push this statue," gasped Wren. "You'll see . . . Everything will be better."

"Go on—cut her throat!" said Shade. "Must I do this for you?"

Oscar glared at Shade, paused for several seconds, then lowered the knife.

"No," said Oscar softly, almost in a whisper.

Shade clenched his jaw, and the muscles in his face rippled with tension. He started to push toward Oscar, through the mass of graylings. But instead of parting to let him go, the graylings braced themselves, hindering his way forward.

"No," said Oscar, much louder this time. He let go of Wren,

turned, and placed his palm against the statue of the old woman.

"Oscar, don't be a fool!" said Shade. He sounded worried now. His eyes were glued to Oscar's palm. "You'll ruin everything we've built. You don't want to do that. You *won't* do that."

Oscar snorted and let his hand fall.

"You think you know graylings so bloody well," he said. "But let me tell you . . . this place is a rat hole. Just like the stinkin' one we came from. And we didn't get to make up the rules in either place. So tell ya what—I'm gonna let Wren show us what she found. How bad can it be? I'm willin' to imagine that just about anywhere else'd be better than here."

"And why'd you keep all hush-hush about this place?" said a grayling girl of ten or eleven. She glared at Shade through pinched eyes. "If there might be a way out, you ought'a said something."

"Now that we seen it, are you gonna vanish us—like you done Nora?" asked another.

Shade tried again to force his way toward Oscar, but the graylings tightened ranks, knives at the ready.

"Stay where you are," said Oscar, glowering at Shade. He pointed at Ember, who had been trying to edge closer as well. "You too."

Oscar turned to Wren. "All right—what now?"

"First, let Alec go," said Wren.

Oscar motioned for the graylings to release him, which they did.

"Okay," he said to Wren. "Now we push these statues."

"*No!*" shouted Ember. She tried to make her way forward

and, once again, the graylings blocked both her and Shade from moving.

Wren grabbed the stone hands on the statue of the old lady and began to push. Alec helped. So did Oscar. They strained their bodies—summoning the strength of their feet, legs, and torso, channeling them into their hands. They gritted their teeth and grunted as they pushed.

The statue of the old woman began to move steadily.

A rumbling echoed through the chamber. Cracks spread along the rock walls of the room, like rivulets of water on a dried streambed. White steam poured from the mouths of the statues. Shade and Ember raced across the room and tried to grab hold of two other statues to slow them down, but it was too late. The statues were moving faster now—building momentum on their own. Alec, Wren, and Oscar stopped pushing but the statues continued to spin.

The grinding noise had become almost deafening. Steam filled the room. The ground shook. Graylings were screaming.

"Wren!" called a voice. "Alec!"

It was Oscar, his face barely visible in the miasma of steam. "We ought'a go!" he yelled.

For an instant, the steam seemed to clear, revealing the empty ramp that rose high above the whirling statues. Shade and Ember were already gone.

"To the Meadow!" screamed Wren.

Alec, Wren, Oscar, and the graylings darted through the moving statues and onto the ramp. The statues were spinning so quickly now that they were a blur of motion. Together, the horde of children clambered upward.

CHAPTER
42

As soon as they emerged onto the Meadow, Wren heard a loud buzzing, like cicadas singing in the evening. There was a crowd in the middle of the Meadow, gathered around the statues. Even from a distance, Wren could see the red tunics of Simon and his men, but not her mother. She broke into a run, pounding her way across the mossy ground. At last she saw Alinka, standing right next to Simon.

"Mother!" Wren yelled. "MOTHER!"

Alinka turned to look at her daughter. Seconds later, Wren was enveloping her in a hug.

"Wrennie," said Alinka. "Oh, Wrennie . . . you're okay." She smiled and ran a hand lightly across Wren's head. "It must've worked—what you did—look." She gestured toward the statues.

Steam was exploding from the statues' mouths in powerful blasts. Wren guessed what this meant—soon millions of dead might be waking from bliss. She spun around to look for Alec, but he was already at her side. Oscar was there, too—along with all of his fellow graylings. They were transfixed by the statues. And, for the first time, Wren noticed that there were members of the Blind in the crowd as well; they were cupping their hands over their ears, as if the sound of the steam was too loud for them to tolerate.

Roaring geysers of humid steam were now screaming from the statues' mouths and forming long, twisting tendrils that rocketed upward and slithered across the sky like great snakes. At last, these serpents of air dove down toward the bliss houses and blew the doors open. The crowd ran to the terrace at the edge of the Meadow to watch.

And then came the scream.

It was a great collective wail of the dead waking.

Millions of people.

All at once.

Alec and Wren heard it only for a second before it became deafening. But they still could feel the power of the noise. It made the air shake and the ground tremble. The vibrations wiggled into Alec's and Wren's bones.

Down below, it was chaos. People poured from the bliss houses and filled the streets. Alec watched with growing alarm. *Where would they all go?* Five centuries of dead people. All waking at once. The thought was staggering, mind-blowing. *Did we make the wrong decision?*

Wren tugged his arm and pointed at the great wall, which curved back and forth, snaking all the way to the far end of the island.

It was fracturing and splitting apart. Cracks raced up its side so quickly that the entire facade seemed to shiver. Dust and pebbles fell away from it and splashed into the moat below.

Oscar stood near the edge of the wall, looking straight down. He stomped his heel into one of the stones along the precipice. It came loose easily. The stone toppled downward, crumbling as it fell. Using his heel, Oscar dislodged another stone—and then another.

For a second, Wren watched Oscar, but then she turned to face the crowd of people and started yelling.

Alec couldn't hear her because his ears were still ringing, but he could read her lips: *Tear it down!* She rushed to Oscar's side and began to help him kick, stomp, and claw at the stonework. Others from the crowd joined them, including Alec, Alinka, Simon, the other soldiers, the graylings, even the Blind. Together, they hurled stones into the moat, making the water churn and foam as if coming to a boil. The image of this reminded Alec of Suns throwing their fearstones into the water at a great, big funeral.

Slowly, the water began to glow, brighter and brighter with each stone that fell. Meanwhile, the streets below continued to fill with crowds. Some people simply gawked at the moat, while others hurried up the stairs leading to the Meadow.

Up above, on top of the wall, Alec and Wren were finally overcome by exhaustion. They staggered away from the precipice and slid to the ground. Alinka sat with them. "You need to rest," she told them. "You've done your part. They can finish without you." And she was right. Soon people were streaming onto the Meadow in droves.

"So many people," said Simon, who was standing just a

few feet away from Alec, Wren, and Alinka. "We'll need to organize them."

"Someone already has," said Alinka.

A procession of sorts had formed—a parade of the dead—and at its head was an elderly man with long, wispy hair that fluttered in the breeze. He drew steadily closer to the terrace; as he did, his features became visible. He had a long nose and silvery eyes that shimmered like shale in a mountain stream.

It was Sebastian Half-Light.

Walking next to him was a small girl with pigtails. Flower's face was solemn, though when she saw Alec and Wren, her mouth curled up into a half smile.

Before greeting Alec or Wren, or so much as waving at them, both Sebastian and Flower walked to the edge of the wall and kicked away a few loose stones.

"Been waiting a long time to do that," said Sebastian.

He then turned to Alec and Wren.

"Well done, you two," he said. "Well done."

Without another utterance to them, he began directing his followers, telling them where to go and what to do.

Flower walked over to Alec and Wren and squatted down next to them. "I still gotta make good on our deal," she said. "Let's go see about that canoe."

# CHAPTER 43

It took a while to get to the cave. The streets were so packed with people that, at times, it was impossible to move. Flower, Alinka, Wren, and Alec clung to one another. Bodies pressed together, as if the buildings were actually inching inward, making the streets narrower and compressing the crowds like the jaws of a giant vise. Flower was worried. "You're gonna suffocate if we don't get you off the streets," she told Alec and Wren. "Follow me." The first chance she got, Flower led them all into a bliss house. It was empty except for endless rows of dangling vines. Flower ushered them into a stairwell. They took it down for several flights, going deeper and deeper.

Alec and Wren stumbled along.

"Do you know where you're going?" asked Alinka.

"More or less," replied Flower.

They exited into a subbasement of the bliss house, and after some searching, Flower eventually found what she was looking for: a tunnel. She had no torch, so they all held hands, and Flower guided them through the darkness. A short while later, they heard the lapping of waves. There was a faint glow in the distance. And then they emerged into the sea cave.

Once inside the cave, Wren and Alec collapsed onto the cool sand. They just meant to rest for a few minutes, but when Flower and Alinka shook them gently awake, there was a look of urgency on their faces.

"What is it?" asked Alec, rubbing his eyes and yawning.

"You slept for a long time," said Alinka. "We didn't want to wake you, but now it's really time to leave."

"Why?" asked Wren groggily. "What happened?"

"The sea has been rising," said Flower. "We had to paddle the canoe out and find a place to stash it." She glanced back to where the mouth of the cave had been. It had vanished beneath the water. Alec and Wren were lying on the highest ground in the cave—the only place that was still dry. "We gotta get out of here, before the water rises any more."

Flower led them back down the darkened tunnel. It was partially flooded, and in several places, they had to wade through pools up to their knees. Eventually, they came upon a stairwell. Water was flowing down it, as if it were a waterfall. They climbed up and emerged onto a flooded street. Sebastian stood there, waiting for them, in water up to his knees. He was holding on to a vine he'd tied to the bow of their canoe.

"Hello there," said Sebastian. The water had crept up his robe, so that it hung heavily over his bony frame. "Ready for a little paddle?"

Wren and Alec barely paid him any attention. They were too busy taking in what surrounded them or—more accurately—

what didn't surround them. The wall was gone. So was the Meadow. Vanished. As if they had never existed.

"What happened?" asked Alec, scratching his head.

"We took it all down," replied Sebastian, eyes twinkling. "We had help, of course. Lots of it. Even so, the serpent drowned fast, in my opinion. Very fast."

"I don't believe it," said Wren.

"Where's all this water from?" asked Alec.

"Some of it is from the moat," replied Flower. "The water rose when the wall came down. But the sea seems to be rising, too."

"Come on," said Sebastian, grabbing the vine tightly and towing their canoe forward. "I'll show you."

They splashed up the flooded street until they reached a wide river, which cut the island in two.

"This is where the wall and the moats used to be," said Sebastian, sweeping his hand across the seascape in front of them. "Now it's, well . . . see for yourself."

Alec and Wren gazed into the depths of the newly-formed river. Everywhere they looked, they saw nearly translucent staircases—thousands of them, it seemed—that started at the water's surface and led down as far as the eye could see. Throngs of people were using them—children skipping lightly and old men creeping one tender step at a time— down, and down, and down.

"The staircases appeared all along the moat, from one end of the island to the other," said Sebastian. "We can't account for everyone, but it appears the island has pretty much emptied out. We're still waiting for a few graylings to report back."

Alec surveyed the banks of the river once more. A few

clusters of people remained on the shore, but everyone else seemed to be making their way into the water and descending the glassy stairs.

"Where do the stairs lead?" Alec asked.

"Someplace else," said Flower, shrugging her bony little shoulders. "That's all we know, but it looks pleasant enough— nice and bright, anyhow. That'll do, seeing as it's been cloudy for the last five centuries. Damn depressing, you know."

Wren continued to stare into the river. There was something about the staircase that was strangely compelling. She felt drawn to them, in the way that one would be drawn to a roaring hearth on a winter night. Eventually she shook her head, as if trying to ward off the power of this spell.

"I think they must lead to the Sunlit Glade and the Moonlit Beach," said Alinka. "We've earned our passage out of Purgatory, just like the Common Book says."

Wren turned to Sebastian.

"Do you think she's right?" she asked, and then fidgeted nervously, waiting for his reply.

Sebastian hesitated.

"Oh, he'll give you some great riddle about the next life and the great unknown," said Flower. "But he doesn't know any better than the rest of us."

Sebastian gave Flower a look, as if he might be cross with her, but then he shrugged. "She's right," he said. "I have no idea. And there's no shame in that."

Wren took a step closer to Sebastian. "How can you be so calm about it?" she asked him. "What if where you're going is worse than this place?" She glanced down into the staircase, then back to Sebastian. "I mean, everyone is just going down those stairs—*blindly*."

"Well, we're all blind," replied Sebastian. "But perhaps not quite as blind as we once were."

Flower shook her head. "Where do you come up with these sayings anyway?" she asked. "Do you have a list of them?"

Sebastian let out a little chortle.

"Where are Shade and Ember?" asked Alec. "What'd you do to them?"

"Nothing," said Sebastian. "They were some of the first people to take the staircases." Seeing Wren's surprised face, he threw his hands up in the air. "What should we have done? Make them stay? No. They wanted a way out, too. They just went about it all wrong."

"That's an understatement," muttered Flower.

"So you just sent them along?" asked Wren. She sighed heavily and looked around, as if to see whether anyone else shared her concern. "So they'll be there, having a good time— or worse yet, bossing people around—when you get to your happy place at the bottom of this river?"

Alinka placed a hand on Wren's shoulder.

"If it truly is a happy place," said Sebastian, "then there'll be no need to boss anyone around or begrudge anyone else their contentment. And if it's not, well, we'll have Flower to set them straight—won't we?"

Flower brushed this off with a smirk and a wave of her hand.

"Enough talking," said Flower. "Let's get the breathers into their canoe while they're still breathers."

# CHAPTER 44

Sebastian handed Wren the vine affixed to the canoe. "Everything is in here," he said. "Though you may not have to climb up the Drain after all." He furrowed his brow. "I hasten to say I don't know whether this will happen right now, *but*, every once in a while, water comes up out of the Drain, like an overflowing bathtub. It's an event of great mystery in Edgeland."

Alec nodded. He had read about this in history books and had always been fascinated—and frightened—by the idea, though he wasn't certain if he really believed it. The idea that the Drain would reverse its flow seemed unimaginable.

"As it so happens, the Drain overflowed just the week before I died," continued Sebastian. "I remember . . . all sorts of debris was brought up by the water—broken planks from funeral rafts, tattered ribbons of cloth, even a few jewels and amulets. When I got down here, well, there was hardly anyone else here. Point is—I'm wondering if the Drain overflows whenever purgatory is emptied."

"What are you saying?" asked Wren. "The water will just carry us back up?"

"That's what he thinks," said Flower. "But I'm a realist. Hold on to the ropes and the grappling hooks. Just in case."

"You should go," said Alinka, nudging Wren's shoulder gently.

Wren shrugged her off.

"Give me another minute," she said, looking down into the boat. She couldn't bear to look up at her mother. "Just . . . another minute."

They all stood in silence for a spell. Up and down the riverbanks, there wasn't a soul in sight. Everyone had gone, it seemed.

Flower finally broke the silence. "I can still go with you to the Drain," she said.

Wren sniffled and shook her head. "We'll be fine," she said. "The Drain isn't hard to find. Even if we don't get out the way Sebastian described, we'll climb." She turned to Alec. "We've come this far, we'll make it out."

Alec made his way over to the canoe and began searching for a paddle.

Wren didn't budge.

Alinka gave her another little nudge. "You have your father's determination," she said. "And it's time you found him, don't you think? Remember, his family lives at the edge of the Songbird district, along a dead-end street lined with juniper trees. That's where you want to go."

Wren nodded, but she couldn't get herself to move toward the canoe.

A shout pierced the silence and everyone turned. Oscar and a group of graylings were running toward them. Oscar arrived first and addressed Flower and Sebastian.

"Everyone seems to be gone," he said. It was as if he didn't quite believe it himself. "Didn't see a soul."

Oscar walked over to Wren.

"Hey," he said. "Do me a favor, would ya? If you ever make it back to Edgeland, maybe you could find my brother and tell him that you saw me . . . and that . . ." Oscar paused and splashed his feet in the water awkwardly. His deep, sunken eyes blinked rapidly. "Just put out your hands, all right?" He took off his leather boot and shook it vigorously, until a few gold coins fell into Wren's outstretched hands. "I found 'em on one of the beaches here. Maybe he can use 'em to get out of the descenders. And tell Joseph, you know, I miss him."

"Of course," said Wren, taking the gold coins.

"One more thing," he said, turning to Alec. "This old guy—a furrier. His name was Azrael, no . . . Isidro. Yes, that was it. He wouldn't stop asking for you. Kept calling your name like mad. Guess he'd heard about everything that happened on the Meadow." Oscar fished a necklace out of his pocket. It was a woven metal rope with an onyx amulet in the form of a wave. Oscar handed it to Alec. "He said he wanted you to have it. Told me to say that you really were the ghost-child after all, whatever that means. Had me say the words a couple times to make sure I got 'em right."

Alec turned the amulet over in the palm of his hand and traced his finger across the wave. Hot tears suddenly filled his eyes. He kept his head down until he'd wiped them away.

"Thanks, Oscar," he said softly.

The silence that followed stretched out for several long seconds. The moment had arrived, and everyone knew it. Wren turned to her mother. Alinka took Wren's hand, raised it to her lips, and kissed it. Then she hugged Wren fiercely.

Wren closed her eyes tight, trying to prolong this moment any way she could.

"Go," Alinka ordered.

Alec and Wren walked to their canoe, clambered over the gunwales, and climbed inside. Wren sat in the stern, Alec in the bow. They watched mutely as the graylings, led by Oscar, walked down the staircase. Then it was Alinka's turn. She looked back just once, tears streaming down her cheeks, then continued down the staircase until her head vanished beneath the water.

Now the only ones left were Flower and Sebastian.

They each gave a little wave, clasped hands, and splashed into the water together. In another time and in another place, they might easily have been mistaken for a grandfather and his granddaughter wading out for an afternoon swim. They continued down the steps, descending into the crystalline depths of the river, until they were nothing but two distant specks.

Alec and Wren kept staring until, in the blink of an eye, the staircases disappeared. Only water was left.

Their boat rose quickly. Alec and Wren took up their oars and started paddling, but it wasn't necessary. The current was now surging toward the Drain. The water was rising so fast that all the bliss houses were soon underwater. Wren used her oar like a rudder, trying desperately to maintain control of the boat. But it made little difference. The current was their master now. It seemed to be drawing them back to the Drain. The canoe crested a curling whitecap, and both Alec and Wren were thrown off their seats, crashing backward into the hull of the boat.

The roar of the Drain was deafening. It grew louder and louder until its thundering presence overwhelmed their thoughts and fears. The boat lurched so violently from side to side that they didn't dare sit up. Instead, they snaked their arms around the wooden pillars that connected the seats to the frame. Alec wanted to reach out to Wren, to grab her arm, but she was too far away.

The canoe rocked back and forth, tossing them against the hull. A giant wave rose from beneath the canoe, lifting it like a twig. The force was so sudden and powerful that Alec and Wren's heads were driven into the gunwales.

Everything went black.

# CHAPTER
# 45

Alec smelled the world of the living before he saw it. Smelled the brine of the sea, the scent of rotting wood, and the oily odor of herring. Then came the sounds: the lull of waves, the caw of seagulls, and beyond it—ever so faintly—the end-of-night bells from Shadow temples.

"Alec?"

He struggled to sit up and realized there was so much water in the canoe that the vessel was almost completely submerged. Far above, the clear, star-filled sky was beginning to brighten with the early light of dawn. Alec turned and saw Wren. She was sitting in the water as well, rubbing the back of her head.

"We're alive," croaked Alec. He coughed and cleared his throat.

A small wave crashed over the boat, filling it so completely that it slid from beneath them and sank into the depths.

Wren looked around as she treaded water, panicked. "Where do we go?" she asked. "We don't want to be pulled back into the Drain."

"There!" hollered Alec. He pointed to a nearby portion of the Ramparts that ran across a small rocky island. It was only twenty feet away. They swam for the island and—to their amazement—reached its shore without feeling the tug of the Drain's current. They dragged themselves onto the wet, pebbly beach, gasping for air.

When they finally looked up, they could see a nearby vent in the wall of the Rampart. It was the same kind of vent they'd been in before, when they were trying to catch Isidro's boat. Water was flowing *out* of it. This could mean only one thing: The Drain wasn't taking in seawater. For the moment, it was still overflowing, like a sputtering fountain. Alec imagined Sebastian Half-Light encountering a similar scene so many years ago, trying to understand why it had happened.

There was an old stairwell, rising from the rocky island, up to the top of the Ramparts. They half walked, half crawled up it. From there, they managed to get their bearings. They were a mile or so from Needle Island, the very place they'd been before falling into the Drain.

They took the Ramparts westward, heading toward Needle Island, whose lighthouse twinkled in the distance. The route was deserted—no sentries, pilgrims, or priests—just the occasional seagull. This was a relief. As far as they knew, the authorities were still looking for Fat Freddy's killer. By now, they might even have identified this person as Wren.

Along the way, they came upon a great clay urn filled with drinking water. Such urns were meant for the pilgrims, so they wouldn't go thirsty while visiting the Ramparts. Inside the urn were two wooden dippers—one marked for Suns and one marked for Shadows. This was typical. The religions did everything they could to keep themselves apart. Given what awaited them down below, it now seemed like an absurd notion. Alec and Wren each took a few tentative sips. They knew if they guzzled it, they would vomit it right back up. The water tasted divine. After some time, they continued on their way.

When they finally reached Needle Island, the sky was markedly brighter. Dawn had arrived. As far as Alec and Wren could tell, they'd been gone for about seventy-two hours—just a single night.

It was almost impossible to fathom.

Their thoughts now centered on Crown, who'd promised to pick them up, at dawn, at this very spot. They sat on the shoreline, rubbing their hands together, trying to keep warm.

"Do you think he'll come?" asked Alec.

"As long as we're right about which dawn it is," said Wren. "For a sunstone he'll be here." She patted the pocket of jewels and sunstones sewed into the lining of her robe. "I've got that and then some." She paused. "You think I'm a thief?"

Alec shook his head. "Jewels, sunstones—it was all trash down there. Whatever you took, no one will miss it." He smiled. "I guess you're rich now."

"I wouldn't say that," said Wren. "I'd say *we're* rich."

Alec shrugged. "Where will you go now?" he asked. "Ankora?"

Wren nodded, scooped up a pebble, and rubbed it between the palms of her hands. Then something caught her attention. "Look," she said, pointing at the water. The current had started flowing back toward the Drain. Gradually, over the next half-hour, they listened to a rumble building as the great waterfall roared back to life and dampened their faces with mist.

"It's back to normal," said Wren.

Alec nodded slowly. Wren was right. Everything was back to normal. *Normal*. That was a crazy notion, wasn't it? Because, really, nothing was the same. Because he now knew what was down there—what awaited him—at the bottom of the Drain. What awaited every living person. For a moment, he tried to envision the island. Was it empty? Had the wall and the Meadow magically reappeared, like some puzzle that resets itself? Or had some new island sprung up in its place? He didn't know. Couldn't know. It was maddening. And then, Sebastian's words came back to him: "I have no idea—and there's no shame in that." *Yeah, great. A lot of help that is.* He pictured Flower rolling her eyes. Then, despite himself, he chuckled.

"What's so funny?" asked Wren.

"Nothing," said Alec, still smiling. "Nothing at all."

He turned his gaze back toward the island of Edgeland. The lanterns on its piers and warehouses twinkled against the muted light of dawn. On the Mount, the spires and belfries of the island's temples sputtered with the flames of the night urns.

Alec quickly spotted House Aron.

He could pick it out easily among the other bone houses. He had been happiest there, not just because Sami Aron valued him, but because he *fit* there. He wasn't just good at what he did. He was suited to it. Just like he was *not* suited for life in the north, with his own family. Now he didn't fit in either place. He had nothing. Well, not nothing.

He glanced back at Wren.

She sat, hugging her knees to her chest, staring off at the island. She'd always liked this moment—just before dawn—when the Suns had not yet emerged and the Shadows traipsed tiredly and silently through the streets. If she ever felt at home on Edgeland, it was now, wrapped in the cool early-morning breeze.

It didn't matter, though. She'd never go back. Well, perhaps she would—if only to deliver Oscar's message and his coins to Joseph—but she wouldn't stay. *Not a chance.* Of course, she wanted Alec to come with her to Ankora, but she felt guilty about this. After all, Alec had a life here and—if he left—he would have to give it all up.

But then Wren wondered whether Alec truly had a choice in the matter. After everything they'd been through—everything they'd seen—could he simply return to House Aron as if nothing had changed? It hardly seemed possible.

Wren reached out and took Alec's cold hand, warming it in her own.

A short while later, a merchant's ship—a schooner with peeling red paint—appeared over the horizon. The vessel moved toward them slowly, fighting the powerful currents of the Drain.

The schooner made its way toward them and dropped anchor. Several deckhands began hustling to lower the mainsail. A short man wearing a three-pointed captain's hat stood at the bow.

Crown.

Wren stood up and waved her arms. Crown saw her and waved back. Soon, a skiff was lowered, with six rowers pulling it deftly toward the lighthouse. A rope tethered the little boat to the schooner to ensure that it was not sucked into the Drain

Wren looked at Alec and tilted her head slightly. "What do you want to do?"

Slowly, he rose to his feet.

"The Desert Lands don't sound too bad," he said. "Besides, I don't think Sami Aron is ready for me to return from the dead."

# EPILOGUE

They stayed in Crown's cabin. For a few gold pieces, Crown was all too happy to move out. His room was spacious—with a large bed and a hefty wooden table and chairs.

The sun was strong on the open seas, and initially they spent a great deal of time belowdecks, resting, eating, and listening to the groan and creak of the ship's old timber frame. To pass the time, Alec sang the lullabies and love ballads that the old washerwomen crooned back on the docks of Edgeland. But no prayers or hymns. Nothing from the bone houses.

The more time he spent on the boat, the more he decided that his former life was over.

What he remembered from that life, more than anything, was how certain he'd been. Certain that House Aron was the greatest bone house. Certain that Suns were keepers of the one true faith. Certain that he was sending the dead to a peaceful resting place. How certain he was. And how wrong. Alec knew every detail of the Sun funeral rites, down to the most obscure furrier hymns, and yet he knew nothing.

At one point, midway through their journey, Crown paid them a visit. When he appeared in their doorway, his face was grave.

"We have a bit of bad news, I'm afraid," said Crown.

"What is it?" asked Wren.

"An old deckhand passed away," said Crown. "Died peacefully enough, in bed, but the men want a funeral—want to send him off to sea on a raft—back toward the Drain."

Wren and Alec looked at each other, but said nothing.

"The man's son is aboard as well—he's the ship's second mate," continued Crown. "He's asking for a proper funeral. Some of the men overheard that you were on the ship," he said to Alec. "They were wondering, well, if you wouldn't mind presiding."

Alec said nothing.

"It would mean a lot to the men," said Crown.

Still, Alec said nothing.

"Alec?" said Wren.

"All right," said Alec, struggling to his feet. "I'll see what I can do."

By the time Alec and Wren emerged onto the deck, most of the crew had assembled. They were gathered around the body of an elderly man, who lay on a raft, which sat on the quarterdeck. Kneeling next to the dead man was his son, the ship's second mate, Able.

"He would've wanted to die at sea," said Able, still staring at his father. "Thing is, I don't even know the words to chant."

"You're a Sun?" asked Alec.

For the first time, Able looked up. "Yeah," he said. "Though we never made it to temple much—neither of us was much for goin' ashore. Don't suppose you could call us believers. Even so, now that he's gone, I'd like to say them words. My father knew them. Didn't know much else, but he knew them words. I remember he said 'em when my uncle passed."

The skin around Able's jaw quivered, the only sign of the grief he was holding in.

"I can help you," said Alec.

"I ain't devout," said Able. His voice cracked for a second. "I ain't been good. Been sailin' and smugglin' my whole life. Never talked to the gods." He looked pleadingly up at Alec. "And they ain't never talked to me."

"That's all right," said Alec. His voice was soft and kind. He paused. "Would you like me to say the prayer?"

"I would," said Able. "I know who you are—know what you do—and I really would appreciate it."

Alec cleared his throat and began to sing, his exquisite and perfectly true voice rising from his lungs and across the decks of the old schooner . . .

*The sun is setting and darkness now comes,*
*Feel the dying light,*
*Bidding the wanderers home from the storm,*
*Warming the faces of friends and strangers,*
*This last day,*
*This last time.*

"Yes," said Able. He looked up at Alec gratefully. Slowly, with great effort, he rose to his feet. "Those are the words I needed to hear."

Alec nodded solemnly and returned to his cabin below-decks.

Several days later, when the sea journey was nearly over, Wren woke from her sleep with a start. She looked around the cabin groggily. Alec's hammock was empty.

Wren stood, dressed quickly, and made her way to the deck. The seas were calm, with only a slight wind pushing the boat toward the Desert Lands. Even though day had not yet broken, the air felt dry—already arid and desert-like. Far up above, the last stars flickered weakly, and the eastern sky had begun to lighten with the promise of dawn.

She found Alec in the stern, pacing back and forth, hands clasped together.

"Up early?" she asked.

He nodded, an uncertain expression on his face.

"I was just thinking about my parents," he said. "They were—*they are*—so proud to be Suns. By now, they probably heard that I fell into the Drain and they think I'm in purgatory, preparing for the Sunlit Grove." A sudden gust of wind made Alec take a step back. "But instead I'm near the Desert Lands, going to Ankora with you."

"Do you want to see them?" Wren asked. "After Ankora, maybe I'll go with you. I've never been up north."

"I don't know," he admitted. "I mean, what would I say?" He exhaled and rubbed his face. "I keep thinking we should tell someone the truth."

Wren snorted. "Would anyone believe us?"

"No," replied Alec. "But it might make me feel better. The truth is, I'm even more scared of dying now than I had been before." The early-morning air was cold, and he felt goose bumps form along his skin. His face was pale against the dim light. "I think a lot about everyone going down those stairs—into the water. They seemed so calm. I wouldn't be that way. I'd be . . ." He shook his head and looked away.

"It wasn't time for us yet," said Wren, placing a hand on his shoulder. "We have more living to do."

"And what if you die first—and you have to go without me?" asked Alec. "What then?"

"Then you'll just do what you always do," said Wren with a smile. "You'll follow me."

"Give me a break," said Alec, pushing her away playfully. She stared at him intently.

"I believe in you," said Wren. "I believe that you are a good person—and there's lots that you can do for people— just like you did for that second mate, Able. You helped him. And you can help others. That's what I believe in."

He took her hand and held it tightly. "That's something, I suppose," he said, looking directly at her. "Isn't it?"

Wren nodded.

The sun peeked above the cloudless horizon: sunrise. Just then, in the distance they could see the contours of land—a series of sloping mounds—the great rolling dunes of the Desert Lands, stretching along the horizon as far as the eye could see.

"Come on," said Wren. "We better get our things. We'll be there soon. Are you ready?"

Alec breathed in slowly. A deep, long breath that curled into the bottom of his lungs. "Yes," he said. "I think so."

**THE END**

# ACKNOWLEDGMENTS

This was the hardest book we ever wrote. When our heroes, Wren and Alec, were lost in the underworld—so too were we. We made it through thanks to the following people.

There were times when we lost faith, but we never doubted our editor, Ari Lewin. When we needed a fresh set of eyes, Amalia Frick answered the call. To Lindsay Boggs, you make the book publishing world spin. To the powerhouse leadership of Jen Besser, Felicia Frazier, and Jen Loja—you're what makes Putnam/Penguin the best! We would also like to thank a host of others in the greater Penguin family, including Eileen Kreit, Julia McCarthy, Emily Romero, Erin Berger, Kara Brammer, Carmela Iaria, Marikka Tamura, Kristin Smith, David Briggs, Emily Rodriguez, Liz Lunn, Cindy Howle, Rachel Cone-Gorham, Anna Jarzab, Madison Killen, Shanta Newlin, Todd Jones, Wendy Pitts, and Helen Boomer.

To Svetlana Katz at WM—your words of advice and encouragement were indispensable. Tina Bennett, as always, was a steady hand. If ever our ship should fall off the edge of the earth and—we'd want Tina at the helm. Thanks also to Alicia Gordon and Erin Conroy for your vision and tenacity in the realm of TV and film.

JAKE: Thanks first to my mother, Tamar Halpern, for always believing in me with your whole heart; and also to my father, Stephen Halpern, for your love and support. To my wife, Kasia Lipska. 10-26-96. I remember that day like yesterday. And many more to come. To my sons, Sebastian and Lucian, every story I tell is really for you. You remain the lights of my life. To Paul Zuydhoek and Mirek Gorski, our conversations about history gave me much inspiration. Betty Stanton, thank you for your magic—Pustefix Bubbles and otherwise. Best wishes to my fellow author: Barbara Lipska! Thanks also to Greg Halpern, Ahndraya Parlato, Witek Lipski, Coach Cheyenne Noble, Susan Clinard, Micah Nathan, Brian Groh, and Emily Bazelon. And, of course, fist-bump to my CF crew, Aaron Poach, Carla O'Brien, Jared Keith, Mike Pozika, Gil Simmons, and Benny Brunson.

PETER: To my wife, Nancy—you are wonderful and supportive and amazing in all ways—that moment you shot me in paintball is the moment that everything changed for the better. To my children—Blaze, Alina, and Sylvie—you make my days sweet. To my mom, Jo Kujawinski, *il arrive parfois que la route soit belle*. Thanks as well to Liza Kujawinski-Behn, Mark Behn, Alex Behn, Clare Behn, Dan Kujawinski, Maureen Finneran, Arlene, Dave, Charla, Brock, Lauren T., Steve, Lauren, Ryan, and Gil Weinsier. And to my old buddies: Joe Napoli, Alastar McGrath, Dan Reichart, Brian Zittel, Marcus Pearl, and Steve Mesler—I'm proud to call you my friends.

# Suns and Shadows

Celia Rose